LULU'S RECIPE FOR CAJUN SASS

SANDRA HILL

SH
BOOKS

PROLOGUE

On the road again...

*L*ouise Rivard was cruising along the Louisiana bayou road in Lillian, her vintage lavender Chevy Impala convertible. Lillian was the name she gave to all her cars. Traded one in, got another, different make, usually a used jalopy in the early days, but still the same name.

But then, in the midst of her reverie, she heard the police siren behind her. Even with two cushions under her butt to compensate for her diminutive (*okay, short, darn it!*) height, she was barely able to see in the rearview mirror. When she recognized the cop in pursuit, she let loose with her version of a curse, "Oh, for the love of Jude! Not again!"

St. Jude, her favorite saint, was the patron of hopeless causes. Not that she was feeling particularly hopeless today, seeing as how she was dressed to the nines, lookin' good, if she did say so herself, and off to that new restaurant, The Mudbug, to have lunch with her niece...well, her niece a couple of times removed or somethin' like that. Mary Lou Lanier, Charmaine's girl, a pre-veterinary student at Tulane, had begged her to meet today. The fact that she insisted on driving from their family ranch up north on a weekday when there were a bunch of mares about to give birth told Louise that it must be something important.

Hard to believe that Mary Lou is a young woman now! My, how time flies by! Or that Charmaine has a baby boy, a toddler, after a twenty-year break since Mary Lou was born! I remember when Charmaine was gettin' married (and divorced) so many times her weddin' cakes scarce had time to go stale, especially to the same man, Raoul Lanier, or Rusty, the sexiest cowboy this side of the Mason-Dixon line. Of course, Charmaine allus did match him in sexiness. She takes after me. Like the time me and Charmaine entered a belly dancin' contest, and Rusty...never mind. Louise's mind wandered a lot these days. She had to concentrate extra hard to keep her focus.

Glancing at the St. Jude bobblehead on her dashboard, she noted that the little statue wasn't even doing the hula. *How fast could I have been goin'?*

She pulled over into the parking lot of Boudreaux's General Store where a sign announced a special on jumbo bags of pork rinds, along with good deals on bait worms, okra, alligator meat, rods and reels, rotten chicken used for catching crawfish, and Tastykakes. She'd have to stop on her way back. The dumb animals who tried to ravage her vegetable garden...possums, raccoons, and the like...had a passion for those crunchy snacks, which she sprinkled around her fenced vegetable patch. She figured if she fed them the piggy treats, they would leave her tomatoes and sweet peas alone. It had worked so far. As for the okra, she had an overflow crop in her garden that she couldn't give away, and any bayou lady worth her salt made her own cakes, thank you very much, Mister Tasty.

She put on her best glare as the copper got out of his vehicle—a dark sedan, unmarked except for the bubble light on top—and strolled up to the driver's side of her car. He wasn't wearing a uniform, but he was a policeman, all right. John LeDeux. A detective who'd transferred last year from the force in Lafayette to Houma. He was her great-nephew, or some such connection; sometimes, Louise forgot the fibs she'd been telling for decades and got her family tree mixed up.

Several faces were pressed up against the window of the store, trying to get a look-see at what she was doing. The nosy posies! Louise still had a snap in her garters, which attracted the menfolk of a certain age and wimmen who wanted to see what she was up to these days, but then, maybe they were ogling her nephew who'd be the first to say he was hotter than asphalt outside a strip club on a summer day. And, yes, the rascal had been a stripper at one time…one very short time, bless his rascally heart. He wore a pure white button-down shirt, open at the neck, blue jeans, a navy sport coat, and dark sunglasses. Didn't matter that there was a bit of gray at the edges of his overlong dark hair, now that he'd hit forty. Hot was hot when it came to Cajun men.

"Tee-John!" That was the name the rascal had been given when he was a little tyke, Small John, before he'd grown into his six-foot frame of male handsomeness. She loved the boy to pieces. "What did I do now? I know I wasn't speedin'."

He leaned against the side of the car, let his sunglasses slip halfway down his nose, and peered down at her. "Can I see your license and registration, ma'am?"

"Pff! I'll give you ma'am! You know darn well I don't have 'em. Where'd you hide them this time anyhow?"

He shook his head as if she were clueless. "You were driving too slow. Buford Doucet called the station to say you had traffic backed up a mile on the bayou road."

"That Buford has some nerve complainin' about me. You oughta check out the old fart when he's drivin' that smelly farm truck of his. And he won't let anyone pass him, either."

"It's a no-passing zone."

She waved a hand dismissively. "Try smellin' cow shit fer a half hour and see if you don't try to go around."

"Tante Lulu! Such language!" Tee-John exclaimed with a grin. Tante was the Cajun word for aunt, which was what everyone called her, even those who weren't blood kin. "Where you off to anyhow?" He gave her appearance a sweeping glance, taking in her neon-blue net driving scarf anchoring down a Farrah Fawcett wig, her heavier-than-usual blonde-toned make-up, thanks to the free samples from Charmaine's beauty salons, and a pale pink tank top with silver sequins spelling out "Sizzling Senior" over hot pink capri pants.

She thought he murmured "Lordy, Lordy!"

"I'm meetin' Mary Lou at The Mudbug." She glanced at the St. Jude watch on her wrist. "And I'm late."

"Well, auntie, shove your little behind over. Looks like I'll be drivin' you into town."

"Why? I kin drive myself," she complained, but she didn't really mind. Sometimes she didn't see the road signs too good. Used to be she could read those old Burma Shave signs from far away. Now...well, they were too faded, even the reproduction ones some local know-it-alls had deemed relics of historical importance. Leastways, that was her excuse for squintin' now and then.

4

"Maybe I just like your company," he said. He adjusted the sunglasses back over his eyes as he opened the driver's door, tossed the cushions into the back, and pushed the seat as far back as it would go.

"How you gonna get back to yer cop car?"

"I'll walk over to Luc's office and shoot the bull for an hour or two, till you're done with lunch. Then, I'll drive you home."

Luc was Lucien LeDeux, his brother and Louise's oldest "nephew." Best known in these parts as the Shark Solicitor because of his talents in the courtroom. If you shot your wife's lover, or were over limit on your possum trappin', or were caught moonin' the mayor, Luc was the lawyer you wanted.

"Doan you have to be workin'?"

"I'm off duty today."

"Ain't it against police rules to be chasin' people with a siren when yer off duty?"

He gave her a look that pretty much asked when he had been one to follow the rules.

He had a point there.

Just then, while Tee-John was making an exaggerated show of turning her car around in the parking lot—it didn't have power steering—old man Boudreaux came out of the store with a broom and proceeded to sweep the sidewalk, which was already clean. *Another nosy posy!* He waved at her, and she waved back.

"Holy crawfish! Don't tell me, that's another one of your beaux from days gone by. Leon Boudreaux is ninety if he's a day, and he's lookin' at you like you're the cream in his café au lait."

She smacked him on the arm. "No, I never dated Leon, but I did almost marry his brother Justin before he went up north to do his doctoring."

"Really? I saw his obit in the *Times-Picayune* last week. A big-time brain surgeon in Chicago, I think it said. Never married."

When he glanced her way, she imagined that his eyebrows, behind the dark glasses, were raised in question.

She just shrugged.

"*Almost* married? Holy *sac-au-lait*! How many marriage proposals have you had, auntie?"

"Seventeen," she answered, without hesitation. "Seventeen serious ones. I doan count all those phony baloney ones where the dumb clucks thought they could get the key to my bedroom with a wink and a pinch."

Tee-John blinked at her. It was always a pleasure to Louise when she could shock her wild nephew.

But then he exclaimed, "Seventeen!"

"What? Why are you so surprised? I've lived a long life."

"That's for sure," he muttered under his breath, then asked, "When was your last proposal?"

"Two weeks ago. Leroy Hamm begged me to marry him, but he's lookin' fer someone to spring him out of the Happy Hours Nursing Home."

Tee-John shook his head, not sure if she was joshing him or not. "I always figured it was your famous dead fiancé that turned you into a spinster, but now I'm wonderin'. This Justin Boudreaux...is he the reason why you never married? Or maybe one of those other seventeen men?"

"None of yer beeswax," she said.

If he only knew!

~

WHEN YOU NEED ADVICE, *go to the opinion goddess...*

Mary Lou had just been seated in The Mudbug, the

new Houma restaurant located on the ground floor of a restored Victorian mansion, hardly having time to check out her surroundings, when her great-aunt arrived. She watched with amusement as the old lady walked across the dining area, wobbling on high-heeled, wedge sandals toward their booth. Her colors shouted va-va-voom.

The small half-circle banquette Mary Lou had chosen was in an alcove at the far side, following the curve of a corner window that overlooked a back courtyard with a fountain and outdoor seating, not yet open to the public. Practically every table or booth the old lady passed had someone calling out for her to stop and chat, usually accompanied by a hug. Many of them, especially the older ones, had used her services as a *traiteur*, or folk healer, over the years.

Or maybe people just wanted to get a closer look at Tante Lulu's outrageous get-up of the day. You never knew what color her hair would be, what kind of make-up she would be experimenting with this week (*can anyone say twenty shades of Maybelline eye shadow?*), or whether her clothing came from Frederick's of the Bayou or the children's section of Wal-Mart—to fit her tiny frame, which seemed to be shrinking by the year, if not the day, bless her heart.

Today she was in blonde mode, a cross between Pamela Anderson and Betty White. Ironically, as over-the-top as her appearance might be to the young crowd, more than one old guy gave her great-aunt a second, and third look, sometimes even a wink.

Kudos to her!

To tell the truth, Mary Lou's very own mother Charmaine was a younger...well, fortyish...clone of Tante Lulu. Charmaine had once self-proclaimed herself in a magazine article, to Mary Lou's pre-teen humiliation, as a "bimbo with a brain." Which was an apt description. Charmaine LeDeux Lanier didn't open a dozen beauty salons and spas on her outrageous looks alone.

Therefore, kudos to her mother, too!

Unfortunately, the apple fell far from my tree, Mary Lou thought, looking down at her faded skinny jeans and sleeveless white blouse. Mary Lou had to think for a moment to recall whether she'd put on any make-up at all this morning, or not. She often forgot as she went about her chores on the ranch, taking care of the horses, or even on the Tulane campus when she rushed to her pre-vet classes.

Yes, she decided, she had put on a little mascara and lip gloss, but her long, chestnut hair was pulled off her face into a simple ponytail. Nothing bimbo or outrageous about her at all. In fact...boring!

She winced at the significance of that last word and felt tears well in her eyes. That's exactly how Derek, her long-time boyfriend, had described her...*boring*...when he'd broken up with her last week.

Immediately, Mary Lou stiffened and willed herself to smile, not wanting to alarm her aunt. She needed to ease into the reason why she'd requested this meeting with the lady known as the Ann Landers of the Bayou.

Standing, she gave Tante Lulu a warm hug and showed her with a motion of her hand that she'd had the waiter place a cushion on the opposite bench seat to compensate for her reduced height. In fact, Mary Lou, who was five-foot-nine, had to lean down to kiss Tante Lulu's cheek. You'd wonder how there could be such a disparity in height among two women in the same family...her mother was tall, too...but then Tante Lulu wasn't really their blood kin, though she considered herself aunt to all the LeDeux. It was complicated.

"Thank you for coming, auntie," she whispered against her powdered cheek.

"Are you kidding?" Tante Lulu said. "I woulda driven all the way up to the Triple L if you'd asked me. Any time, sweetie."

"Oh, no! I would never ask you to drive that far. Besides, the ranch is a madhouse today with preparations for tomorrow's big birthday bash. You are coming, aren't you?" Her aunt had to be wondering why Mary Lou couldn't have waited until tomorrow to discuss whatever she had to discuss, but Mary Lou wanted privacy for what she had to say, and there would be little of that at home.

"I wouldn't miss it. I'm comin' with Luc and his family in that new SUV of his. Gotta have room fer my Peachy Praline Cobbler Cake. Oh, I know there will be other cakes…in fact, five birthday cakes, but—"

"—it's not a party without your Peachy Praline Cobbler Cake," Mary Lou finished for her, with a smile.

"Yep. I'm hopin' my cake will sweeten up those mommies who're still a little bit mad at me."

"A little bit" was an exaggeration. More like a lot. But then, Tante Lulu was always pissing off one person or another as she breezed through life like a mini bayou bulldozer. To say she had no filter when expressing an opinion would be a gross understatement. On the other hand, the people she pleased, those who loved and admired her, well, they far outweighed the others. She was a gem…flawed, garish to some eyes, but a treasure just the same.

If only I could…never mind. That can wait.

As to the family's current gripe…tomorrow's party marked the one-year birthdays for five boy babies, all born on the same day, to LeDeux family members: Timothy, or Timmy, to Mary Lou's mother and father, Charmaine LeDeux and Raoul Lanier; Christopher, or Chris, to Uncle

Luc and Aunt Sylvie LeDeux; Rafael, or Rafe, to Uncle Remy and Aunt Rachel; Sebastian, or Seb, to Uncle René and Aunt Val; And Gabriel, or Gabe, to Uncle John and Aunt Celine. The ladies, and the men, too, for that matter, all blamed Tante Lulu for their late-in-life pregnancies, something to do with a casually tossed out wish by Tante Lulu to St. Jude that there would be more babies in the family. Or maybe it had just been a sigh. Her aunt's connection to the saint was known to be powerful. For a long time after the mass pregnancy announcement, women throughout the bayou steered clear of her aunt for fear she would look at them in a certain way.

Actually, there would be seven birthday cakes, to include Uncle Dan and Aunt Samantha's twin boys who'd been born two months earlier than the others. They were named David and Andrew, called the DNA twins because of their initials. A bit of Cajun or medical humor there, considering that Uncle Dan was a doctor.

With all the extended family and friends, at least a hundred people were expected to attend. Her daddy had started the coals for his humongous barbecue pit this morning. A half steer would cook slowly for at least twenty-four hours, with the promise of fork-tender steaks and ribs for the party. The sides would be brought by all the attendees.

Even her celebrity cousin Andy LeDeux, best known by the nickname "Candy Andy," a hotshot New Orleans Saints football player, planned to stop by. Some of the cowboys on the ranch would have to do double duty as security around the periphery of the ranch to keep away the fans. Same went for the news media who'd gotten a whiff of Andy's possible trade to a Yankee team. God forbid! The South would rise again if that happened.

She and Tante Lulu placed their orders for sweet tea,

crawfish étouffée, Creole sunburst salads, and a salty caramel bread pudding which they would share. The waitress paused before leaving and asked, "Are you Tante Lulu?"

"I am, dear. Why do you ask?"

"My mama, Eveline Foucet, swears by your diaper rash ointment. Says it's better than anything you can buy in the store. My baby has a bad rash that just won't go away. The poor thing cries all night."

Tante Lulu nodded and said, "You come to my cottage later today, and I'll have the salve ready fer you. I live about a mile past Boudreaux's General Store out on Black Bayou Road. Do you know where that is?"

"I do. Thank you so much!"

"And tell yer mama to stop by anytime. My fig tree is about to burst with fruit, and I recall how Evie allus had a hankerin' fer fig jam."

When the waitress was gone, Mary Lou looked at her aunt. "What's in your salve that makes it so special?"

"Gator spit."

Mary Lou wasn't sure if she was serious or not. But then, it didn't matter. Tante Lulu was Tante Lulu. Mary Lou wouldn't put anything past her.

While they dined, they chatted about family, Tante Lulu's continuing herbal healing business, Mary Lou's studies, and Uncle René's band, The Swamp Rats, which was planning a concert next month for Save the Bayou, an environmental group that was battling the oil industry on the gulf. Her aunt was as alert and funny, as ever, thank God!

"I hear that louse, Valcour LeDeux, has got another girl pregnant. At his age! They oughta chop off his pecker and pickle it in a Mason jar and send it to Ripley's Believe It or

Not. I'd do it myself, except I wouldn't want to touch the slimy thing. Eew!"

"Auntie!"

"Sorry. I forgot, he's yer granddaddy."

"It's not that," Mary Lou said, laughing. "I hardly ever see him. It's what you said...that word."

"What? Pecker? I coulda said somethin' worse."

"I know, I know. Please don't."

Mary Lou knew that Tante Lulu had hated Valcour LeDeux for a long, long time. Everyone knew that. In fact, when Mary Lou's uncles Luc, Remy, and René were boys, they often fled the drunken rages of their father, running to the bayou cottage of Tante Lulu, who was in some convoluted way their aunt, or great-aunt, or something. Tante Lulu claimed he was an egg-suckin' dawg from the first she met him. And the shelf life on Tante Lulu's grievances against Valcour was like forever, but then he kept adding more chits onto his bad boy/man tab. Mary Lou was aware of four legitimate children born to two wives, one deceased and one hanging on by her expensive sculptured nails, but more and more illegitimate ones kept coming to light over the years. Mary Lou's own mother, Charmaine, was one of the illegitimate ones.

It didn't help Tante Lulu's opinion that Valcour was also in bed with the oil companies.

By the time they finished their meal and were sipping at cups of café au lait, Tante Lulu, wise old owl that she was, decided that enough was enough. "No more beatin' around the bush," she said, "Obviously, you have a problem that only I can solve; otherwise, you would've saved the small talk fer tomorrow at the birthday bash."

To tell the truth, Mary Lou was having second thoughts about unloading her issues on the old lady. "Well, actually, it's nothing to bother—"

"Pff! Thass why God put me here. To be bothered. Thass why he assigned St. Jude to be my partner." Tante Lulu beamed with encouragement. "Doan matter whether it's big or small. There's somethin' troubling you, girl, and I'm here to help."

Immediately, tears welled in Mary Lou's eyes. *She's pulling out the St. Jude card. Must be she thinks I'm hopeless. I am!* Mary Lou wailed inwardly.

Tante Lulu reached two hands across the table, squeezed one of Mary Lou's, and continued to hold on. "Tell me, honey."

"Derek dumped me," she confessed on a sob, then immediately lowered her voice when she noticed a couple at a nearby table look their way.

Tante Lulu nodded. "I wondered why you didn't mention him. And you're not wearing that friendship ring."

"Promise ring," Mary Lou corrected, then realized that it didn't matter. The ring and the promise were gone.

"You were keepin' company with that boy fer a long time," her aunt pointed out.

"Yep. Two years. Ever since we were seniors in high school."

The old lady narrowed her eyes suddenly, which caused the mascara clumps to stick together. "Did he cheat on you?"

"No, no," Mary Lou said. "Not that I'm aware of. No, he said I've become...*boring*."

Tante Lulu stared at her for a moment, then burst out laughing. "Girl, I thought it was something serious, like bein' preggers. You aren't, are you?"

"No!" Mary Lou exclaimed.

"Aw, shucks! I was kinda plannin' on convertin' my spare bedroom into a nursery fer you and the baby."

"I am not pregnant," Mary Lou declared emphatically.

That's all she would need, for her mother to get wind of a rumor about her only daughter about to make her a grandmother. And, frankly, Mary Lou was rather offended that Tante Lulu would think she was that dumb. "I'm on the pill, auntie."

Tante Lulu put her hands on her ears. "Doan be tellin' me stuff like that."

Mary Lou was surprised, continually, by the old lady's conflicting ideas. She could be as outrageous as any hell-raising senior citizen, a feminist from way back, but then adhere to her strict Catholic opinions on other things, like birth control.

"Anyhow, being boring *is* serious," Mary Lou said, bringing the subject back around. "The ultimate insult, I think."

"Boring, huh? Thass one thing no one has ever said about the women in this family."

Mary Lou shrugged. "Guess I'm the exception."

Tante Lulu studied her appearance, tapping a fingertip against her lips which were now minus color except for a red line around the edges. Mary Lou resisted the temptation to lean forward and use a napkin to wipe off the excess.

"Well, that just dills my pickle! You're a beautiful girl, Mary Lou, and if brains were leather, that Derek wouldn't have enough to saddle a pissant," Tante Lulu concluded, getting a bit red in the face. "Mebbe yer hair could be fluffed up a bit, and it wouldn't hurt to add a bit of rouge to yer cheeks, and, holy moley, tart up yer clothes once in a while, but other than that, that boy had no bizness callin' you boring."

"Is that all?" Mary Lou should have been offended, but it was hard to take Tante Lulu's jibes to heart when she meant well. "Actually, I don't think it's my physical appearance that he means as boring. More my personality." She turned on her male voice and imitated Derek by husking out, "All you talk about, Mary Lou, is horses, horses, horses. I swear, honey, you'd live in a stable if you could. And all you ever want to do is ride, ride, ride. Not that I don't like a certain kind of riding. Ha, ha, ha! Think about it, sweetheart, you look down on my frat parties, but you're the first one at a barbecue at some shit-stinky ranch or out roping or branding the animals. Be careful, sweetheart, or you're gonna start lookin' like a horse."

Tante Lulu's jaw dropped and she just stared at her for a moment. Then, she said, "What a schmuck! Did it ever occur to him that all he talks about is football? To some of us, tossing a ball around and men tacklin' men to break their bones fer fun is bor-ing. And all those bulgy steroid muscles! Do they wanna look like Popeye? Eew!"

Tante Lulu had a point there. Derek played football for Tulane, and he spent all his spare time watching NFL games on TV or working out with weights, sometimes both at the same time.

"You never did like Derek, did you? I always figured it was because he wasn't Cajun."

"Nope. There are plenty of good non-Cajun men out there. But I suspicioned early on that he was using you to get close to yer cousin Andy. Mebbe get an in with the Saints' big brass."

Mary Lou felt her face flush. That thought had occurred to her, too.

"Not that he wasn't attracted to you and all," her aunt added quickly. "More like he was lookin' fer a little lagniappe, along with the sex." In Cajun land, lagniappe was the little something extra a merchant threw in with a customer's purchase. "Ain't nothin' wrong with a little hanky panky. I never did go for that, 'Why buy the cow when you kin get the milk fer free?' To me, it's jist as easy to say, 'Why buy sausage when steak is on the menu?' What's good fer the goose and all that!"

"Tante Lulu!" Mary Lou exclaimed again. You couldn't say the old lady wasn't blunt...and possibly right. And wasn't it odd how her language fluctuated from almost illiterate to highly intelligent, practically from sentence to sentence? Did she do it on purpose, to give the wrong impression, so she could then zap a person with some wisdom? Probably.

"I'm too old to waste time on pretendin' I doan know what you young folks do. Old folks, too, fer that matter. But thass beside the point. Did you tell yer mother about Derek bustin' up with you? Betcha she'd have some good advice, specially since she was a Miss Louisiana at one time and broke more hearts than the shredding machine at Whitman's Sampler the day after Valentine's."

Mary Lou just blinked at that long spiel, but then she said, "I'm not that crazy...or desperate. If I told Mom, she'd blab to Dad, and you know what he'd do? He'd go after Derek with a cattle prod. I overheard him telling Uncle Luc one time that if any guy hurt his little girl, meaning me, he'd shoot his balls off." Uncle Luc had three daughters, and was always complaining about how they were giving him premature gray hairs, but he'd agreed with her father.

"Yep. You are yer daddy's girl. Allus have been, from the moment he first saw you in the hospital. He cried when he held you fer the first time. Did you know that?"

Mary Lou did know that. Tante Lulu had told her about it at least a hundred times. "I never get tired of hearing about Daddy's love for me, and Mom, and the brat," which was the affectionate name she'd given the new baby, Timmy. It was embarrassing to see how her father looked at her mother sometimes, his heart in his eyes, as old as they both were…almost fifty, for heaven's sake!. But that's the kind of love she'd been looking for, hoping for, with Derek. And that wasn't so unreasonable, dammit! She and Derek had been a couple for years now, and he said he loved her. They'd even talked about marriage sometime in the future…the far future, after graduation, but still…

"So, what do you want now? To get Derek back, or to move on? I got advice that could go both ways."

"I'm not sure. I do love him. On the other hand, I'd like to show him that I can do better."

Tante Lulu nodded.

"You really could help me?"

"For sure, darlin'."

"How?"

"Well, it's obvious," Tante Lulu shook her head sadly, causing the Farrah Fawcett wig to go a bit lopsided, "you've lost something important, and I don't mean the schmuck."

Mary Lou tried to laugh, but it came out as a choke. "What?"

"The thing all bayou gals are born with."

"What?" she repeated dumbly.

"Cajun sass."

*In Tante Lulu's world, **there's a recipe for everything…***

Some folks would discount Mary Lou's heartache as young love that would soon pass, like wind in the bowels, or a bad hair day. They would pat her on the back in a patronizing way and say, "It's not like you have cancer or polio or a bad case of the swamp runs, honey chile." Then there were those dimwits that would say, "Time, the great healer, is your friend; you'll forget that loser quick as spit." Or Louise's favorite: "Men are like buses. You miss one, and another will be along in five minutes, sure as Bourbon Street sin."

Louise didn't say any of those things. After all, she'd been the same age as Mary Lou when she'd fallen in love with Phillipe Prudhomme, then lost him the next year in the big war. More than fifty years later, and her heart still ached for him every single day.

"Oh, auntie!" Mary Lou said with a laugh and reached across the table to squeeze her hand. "You are such a treasure!"

"'Course I am." She preened.

"Where do you come up with this stuff?"

She stopped preening. "Stuff? This ain't stuff. It's pure, guar-an-teed bayou wisdom."

"There's no such thing as Cajun baby girls having a gene for sass," Mary Lou said in a gentle tone, so as not to offend.

Hah! It would take a lot more than that to offend her.

"Genes, smenes! Thass all you know, girl. They're there, all right. The lucky females let it shine right outta their skin, practically from the time they leave the crib. Those are the ones that bat their flirty little eyelashes and turn their daddies into butter. But some gals hold it in. Like constipation. Others jist need a jolt to trigger it loose, like you and me."

"You?"

"Yep. For a long time, years after my Phillipe was gone, I jist wallowed in my miseries. Dint care 'bout my appearance. Heck, I never went out anywhere to be seen."

"Didn't you have to work?"

She shook her head. "No jobs were available, lessen I went into Nawleans to my old job as a typist. But I dint have the energy to make the effort. Plus, I would have had to do my hair and press my clothes. In the end, it was easier to jist sleep way too much, 'cept when Mama dragged me out into the swamps in her pirogue to gather herbs fer her healin' business."

"At least you had that saving grace. Learning to be a folk healer, even if it was against your wishes in the beginning."

Louise was pleased that Mary Lou was following her story so closely, and seemed to understand. She was a smart girl, way too smart for that Derek dope. "Then my Mama died of the cancer and left me with little Adèle, my brother Frank's daughter, to care for."

"Adèle? That was Uncle Luc, René, and Remy's mama, right?"

"Right. Adèle was only five at that time, though, and a handful. Believe me, a toddler runnin' wild with snakes and gators nearby dint allow fer no wallowing. I had no choice but to straighten up and take responsibility."

"So that was your trigger?"

Louise shrugged. "The first of many."

"I know you're trying to be helpful, auntie, but our situations are entirely different. My being boring and unable to hold onto my boyfriend is nothing compared to your grief."

"Grief is grief. The cure is the same."

Mary Lou arched her brows in question. "To pull up my big-girl panties?"

"So to speak. You gotta remember that a dash of Cajun sass kin go a long way to cure jist about anything."

Mary Lou groaned. "*That* again!"

"Always *that*, sweetie. But not to worry. I have the recipe."

"You have a recipe for Cajun sass?" Mary Lou laughed.

Did she think this was a joke? Not to Louise. "Of course. Ain't that what I been tryin' to tell you?"

"You have?" Mary Lou hit the side of her head with the heel of one hand and smiled. "And the ingredients are…?"

Louise could tell that the girl was still an unbeliever.

"SASS. Style, Attitude, Smarts, Stubbornness. Fer a start. 'Course, there are lots of other things…the spices. Like bravery, focus, and optimism."

Mary Lou laughed out loud. "You're serious!"

"Aren't you glad you came to me fer help?"

Just then, Tee-John walked up. "What's taking you so long, old lady? I've been sitting in the parking lot, baking my ass off, waiting for you."

"I thought you were going to Luc's office."

"I did, but he's in court today. You about talked out?"

"Doan be such a grump."

"Hi, Uncle John."

He sat down and began to eat the remainder of the bread pudding. "Yum!" he said, then, "You two were laughing like hyenas when I came in. What was so funny?"

Mary Lou used a napkin to wipe at the tears of mirth that still rimmed her eyes. "We were just talking about recipes," she told him.

"Recipes? I like the sound of that." He turned his attention to Louise. "Hope it's the recipe for Hot Pepper Jam. I ran out of that batch you gave me for Christmas."

Tee-John had a fondness for the preserves that she made with habaneras and rhubarb served over cream cheese-slathered crackers.

"No, Tee-John, this is an entirely different recipe. It's one of those change-your-life formulas."

"Well, hell's bells! Count me in. I'm always up for a new experience."

"Celine would have something to say about that," Louise said.

"Only good things," Tee-John protested. "My wife loves all the new experiences I bring her way." He waggled his eyebrows for emphasis.

"Like the time you were a stripper? Or the time you went to the underwear-optional party? Or when you drove my convertible into Lake Pontchartrain?"

"Those were all before Celine and I got together. So, they don't count." He sat back and grinned with satisfaction, as if he'd won the argument.

The fool!

Mary Lou's head was swiveling back and forth as she witnessed this exchange, probably learning a few things she didn't need to know about her uncle.

"Anyways, the recipe Mary Lou and I were discussing is fer women only."

"Aw, shucks!" he said. But then, as he thought for a moment, he added, "I can't imagine any time when you needed a change-of-life experience, auntie. Seems to me, you've always been a bayou gal, born, bred, and stay the same till you're pushin' up daisies...or okra."

"You have no idea," she said. "Now, skedaddle. Mary Lou will drive me home so we kin continue our discussion. I gotta give her the exact recipe."

She noticed Tee-John and Mary Lou exchanging a look, probably wondering if she was losing it. People had been giving her that look for decades now. That didn't matter to Louise. She needed a little time to recollect that period in her past when she'd been at her lowest and felt the need to call on her bayou background...to garner her...yes, her Cajun sass.

Of course, there had been a man involved.

CHAPTER 1

Bayou Black, 1951...

Don't get around much anymore...

*L*ouise stepped out the back door and off the porch of her cottage, then flinched as the afternoon sun hit her with a wallop of steam heat.

Even though it was early August in the South with its seasonal high temperatures, she was surprised to find it hotter outside than it was inside where she had a five-gallon pot on the kitchen stove simmering up a new batch of croup syrup. A wave of summer flu had swept through the bayou these past few weeks, leaving her sorely depleted of the highly effective, homemade cough medicine. Fortunately, it appeared to be the tail end of the mini epidemic.

Putting her hands to the small of her back, she arched out a few of the kinks and sighed. What she really needed was to crawl into bed and take a nap. Or a bubble bath would be nice. She probably smelled as bad as she looked.

If only she had the time!

Thou hadst time to drink two cups of coffee this morning. Thou hadst time to take the Lord's name in vain when chasing that swamp creature. But, forget thy stink, didst say thy morning prayers? No. Ah, the priorities of God's children!

St. Jude, the patron saint of hopeless cases, was Louise's favorite, ever since he'd saved her from a soul-rending despair six years ago. But then he'd stuck around, speaking to her in her head on occasion...like now. To say he was a royal pain in the patoot at times was an understatement. But still, she couldn't ignore him. Oh, no! One did not ignore a celestial messenger.

Okay, okay. I'll shower before Adèle wakes up and then say my prayers.

Priorities again!

She made a growly noise. *Got it. Prayers first.*

Bless you, child.

Hah!

In Louise's defense, it had been the day from hell (*forgive my language, Mister J, if that sounds sacrilegious*), starting with two of her late mother's customers showing up practically at the crack of dawn needing medicinal herbs, not for the croup, but for equally desperate issues... to them, leastways.

For some reason, without her actually making a decision, people had assumed she would take over as Bayou Black's only *traiteur* when her mother died last year. Although she'd learned much at her mother's side about folk-healing herbs, she was still winging it in many regards. For example, this morning, even though she had the receipt book that had been passed down through three generations of Rivard females, it had taken what seemed like forever, not helped by her sleepiness, to match up the recipes with the dusty bottles on the pantry shelf for two different customers suffering from migraines and male genital rash.

Another job for her when things settled down—organizing Mama's "pharmacy."

More priorities! St. Jude said.

Louise rolled her eyes.

After her customers had left, she had to use a broom to chase a baby alligator out of her blueberry patch and back into the stream where its anxious mama, whom she had named Gloria, was no doubt waiting to take a bite of some tasty human flesh. Her five-year-old niece Adèle had gotten so hyped up by the encounter...jumping up and down with excitement, giggling, screaming, wanting to pet the stupid thing...that it had taken Louise more than an hour afterward to get the by-then weepy, fussy child down for her usual nap. Two loads of laundry were waiting for her, and she still had an order of fresh fruit and vegetables to deliver to Boudreaux's General Store, a small but essential source of income to supplement her folk-healing proceeds.

Louise was only twenty-six years old, but she felt like seventy-six most days. And it wasn't just physical exhaustion that wore her down. It was the never-ending grief of losing her father, her fiancé Phillipe, her brother Frank, and her mother, but mostly Phillipe. And the responsibility of raising her daughter while pretending the child was actually her niece.

Louise sighed again and picked up a large, oval wicker gathering basket by its handle and walked over to the fig tree where she began to gather the ripe fruit. She would need to make fig jam for herself, but this first harvest would be for sale. Every penny counted these days. She was saving to buy new tires for her jalopy, which she'd named Lillian two years ago after trading in the car she'd inherited from Phillipe when it had broken down once too many times.

Once she dumped the figs into two sturdy cardboard tomato boxes, she moved to the vegetable garden. Tomatoes, green peppers, scallions, string beans, okra, several varieties of lettuce, squash, zucchini, and snap peas soon filled two more boxes on the porch. She was back in the garden, bent over, pulling out carrots by their green fleecy tops from the loose soil when she heard a motor vehicle approaching, then pulling into the clamshell driveway behind her at the side of the cottage. She didn't straighten and look back...not at first, figuring it would be another of the *traiteur* customers seeking some herbal remedy.

When she did glance back over her shoulder, she saw a man leaning against the front of a short-bed truck, arms folded over his chest, staring at her bottom which was pretty much aimed in his direction.

Men! Pfff! Wearing loose bib overalls over a short-sleeved man's undershirt, both of which once belonged to her brother, belted with a twisted scarf at the waist and the ankle cuffs rolled up to mid-calf, she knew her figure was nothing to garner any kind of attention. Heck! Even naked, or wearing fancy lingerie, she was no voluptuous pin-up these days, if she ever had been, never mind those posters she'd done for Phillipe when he'd been stationed overseas. No breasts or hips to speak of, and only five-foot-three on a good day. As for her hair, which was a frizzy dark cloud about her face in this humidity, she couldn't recall if she'd even brushed it this morning. Usually, she tucked it under one of those red farmer's handkerchiefs, Rosie the Riveter style. And the sun was doing a great job of turning her skin not to a burnished gold but a red raspberry tone.

And yet this man had a grin tugging at his lips and his

eyes sparkled mischievously as he perused her with bold appreciation.

Men! she thought again. *They can be aroused by a tree limb if it's the right shape.* She straightened and turned, planting her hands on her hips. It was then that she realized he wasn't looking at her with admiration, but rather amusement. Or indifference.

The man was not attracted to her.

More than that, he thought she was funny.

For some reason, that annoyed her. Not that she was attracted to him. Still, no woman wanted a man to laugh at her.

On closer scrutiny, she admitted that he was good-looking in a lean, lazily sexual way. Who was she kidding? The man was ten kinds of sexy. And he knew it, if the spark in his whiskey-hued eyes was any indication. Light brown, overlong hair stuck out from under a battered, but jauntily tilted, straw Fedora. A faded plaid, button-down shirt hung over the slim hips of black work pants, ending in scuffed leather boots. He was clean-shaven, but dark whiskers already shadowed his face, not in an unappealing way. He appeared tall, but was probably under six feet.

There were plenty of men about since the war ended five years ago. Some of them were shell-shocked, and a few had lost a limb or two. But mostly the men of the bayou who'd returned provided a vast array of handsome Cajun masculinity to the girls who'd stayed behind.

But none of that mattered. A man was the last thing she needed in her complicated life, and, really, no one could ever take Phillipe's place. "Can I do somethin' for you?" she asked testily when he continued to just stare at her, and say nothing.

Which, of course, was a poor choice of words.

"Oh, *mais oui*, darlin'," he said with an exaggerated

Cajun accent, pushing away from the truck. Before she had a chance to be offended by his innuendo, which was misplaced considering his lack of attraction, he added, "My father sent me to pick up a delivery."

"Your father?"

"Joseph Boudreaux. I'm his older son, Justin. I believe you know my younger brother Leon."

Just then, she noticed the logo on the door of the truck. "Boudreaux's General Store." She stepped forward out of the garden, clapping her hands together to remove some dried mud. *Better not shake hands*, she thought, even before his upper lip curled with distaste at her grubbiness.

"I was fixin' to deliver the produce later this afternoon."

He shrugged. "I had to be out this way, so Dad asked me to stop and save you the trouble." It was obvious the side trip was not a welcome one.

She motioned him toward the back porch. "Come, you, sit down while I get the rest of my order ready. Would you like a glass of sweet tea while you wait?" *Or some sour lemonade to match your mood?*

He frowned as he watched a gator floating down the bayou stream. Possibly, Gloria, the baby's mother from this morning, but, no, this one was much bigger. Had to be a male. Maybe Gloria's boyfriend. She didn't know why Justin should be frowning, though. Gators and other wild creatures were a fact of life on the bayou.

"I'd love a cold drink," he said, once the gator was out of sight, then sank down into one of the two high-backed rocking chairs. There was a two-person swing at the other end of the porch.

"Be back directly," she told him and went inside to wash her hands and turn down the heat on the stove. Before she returned outside to pack up the rest of the produce, she checked on Adèle, who was thankfully still knocked out on her cot from her energetic morning. As Louise had suspected, when she glanced in the mirror, she saw that she was a mess. There were even some twigs in her hair. Oh, well. She wasn't out to impress anyone...least of all a full-of-himself Cajun stud.

"Can I help you?" he asked half-heartedly a short time later as he sipped at his drink, his long legs extended and crossed at the ankles.

"No. I'm fine. I'll be toting in lots more over the next few weeks, gettin' ready for Labor Day weekend."

He nodded, and contented himself with observing her packing up more of the vegetables into boxes, along with a passel of fresh-cut sunflowers which she tied with a string into a half dozen clumps and slid into a paper sack. Sometimes folks bought a bouquet or two on a whim, though she wasn't about to explain that to him.

"Who is that?" he asked, holding up a paper napkin with a face imprinted on it, then pointing upward to the wind chimes hanging from the porch ceiling with bronze discs displaying the same image.

"St. Jude."

He arched his brows in question. "You mean the traitor, the guy who betrayed Jesus."

"No. Jude Thaddeus, the brother of James, was an apostle. He's often confused with that other apostle Judas Iscariot, the bad guy," she told him. She waved at the napkin and wind chime and explained, "Maisie Fontenot got them for me when she went to Rome last year. She also bought me a St. Jude umbrella."

"Isn't Jude the patron saint of hopeless cases?"

She felt her face heat. Why did she always have to defend her devotion to St. Jude, like it was weird of something? "Yes."

"Are you feeling hopeless?"

"Not now. But there have been times in my past."

He chuckled. "Maybe I could use a little of his help in preparing for my medical board exams."

He was probably joking. Still, she offered, "I could give you a medal." She had more than twenty left from the stash she'd bought at a church rummage sale last year.

"Thanks, but I'll pass for now." She must have given him a dirty look because he added, "I'm not much for wearing jewelry."

She thought about warning him not to annoy the saint, but then St. Jude whispered in her head, *Not to worry, child. I am overburdened with prayers for help these days.*

Suddenly, Justin scrooched up his nose, looking toward the open door of the cottage. "What is that godawful smell?"

At first, she thought he referred to her body odor and barely restrained herself from sniffing at an armpit. But then she noticed him looking toward the cottage interior. "Croup cough syrup." She'd become immune to the pungent odors after all this time.

"You're making medicine? Isn't that...illegal?"

"I don't call it medicine. Folk healing relies on herbs and such." Although the new FDA regulations under the Durham-Humphrey Act didn't speak to folk medicine, it clearly tried to outlaw any drugs that could be harmful or habit-forming without a physician's prescription. Which wasn't a problem for Louise. But it was best to be careful. The last thing she needed was some FDA person snooping into her business.

He frowned and gave her a skeptical look. "That's split-tin' hairs, don't you think?"

"What are you...the medicine police?" *Lordy, Lordy, could he be FDA?*

"No, but I am a doctor, or almost a doctor."

She stopped loading her produce and looked to him with question. Now that he mentioned it, she recalled Leon mentioning a brother, about four or five years older than the two of them, who was studying medicine. "Almost?"

"I'm doin' a residency this summer at Charity Hospital in Nawleans. Hope to finish up by next month."

"And then?"

He shrugged. "Not sure. Maybe continue my studies with a specialty. Or take a job with a family practice for a year or two, then decide if I want to branch off."

"Back here in the bayou?"

"I'm not sure. There are some excellent hospitals up north where I could learn a lot. It would be an honor to be asked to join them."

"And are there no 'excellent hospitals' in the South?"

"Of course. It just depends on what specialty I choose, if I choose a specialty."

"And in the meantime you're deliverin' vegetables. And gettin' all hoity-toity over my cough syrup."

He laughed, and, boy oh boy, his handsomeness amped up to about too-hot-to-handle. "No, I was just helpin' Dad on my afternoon off work."

Good for you, daddy's boy, she thought. *But you probably hoped to hook up with some beautiful bayou gal along the way. Instead, you got stuck with me.*

A grin twitched at his lips as if he knew what she was thinking.

The fathead.

His head shot up as if a sudden thought had come to him. "Please don't tell me you were doling out medicines during that recent Asian influenza epidemic?"

She bristled. Something about this almost-doctor really got her dander up and she exploded, "No, I did not. Me, I am not so much a fool that I would think I have a cure for some strange virus. If I did, I would be famous and rich as one of them Rockerfellers, now wouldn't I? But what I did do was give my customers herbal remedies to relieve shortness of breath or fever for the summer flu that hit here, not an epidemic. And, yes, I kept my pantry cleaner than a bleach factory, cleaner than some doctor's offices I been in."

He was clearly amused by her reaction, probably an overreaction, to his insulting words, which might very well have been teasing. She didn't know him well enough to tell the difference.

"Where at you studyin' medicine?" Sometimes Louise deliberately dumbed down her language when she was around people who considered themselves superior intellectually.

"Up north. Harvard."

Well, you couldn't get any higher intellectual reputation than Harvard, she supposed. "Well, la dee da! So, you become Yankee now?"

He smiled. "Hardly. You jump to a lot of assumptions, my dear."

He even sounded uppity, not at all Cajun-ish. "You know what they say about Yankees, dontcha? They're like hemorrhoids. A pain in the be-hind when they come south, but a relief when they go back up."

A slight tic at the side of his closed lips was the only indication she'd pricked his pride. "That joke is as old as time."

She shrugged. "If the boot fits, no sense throwing it out."

But then he smiled. "I can't believe we're arguing about old jokes. You're a little bit snippy, darlin'. Did I say somethin' to offend you?"

Hah! He thought he could toss out a "darlin'" with a sexy smile and suddenly become Cajun-ish. "Is the sky blue, *darlin'*? Do birds fly?" she inquired sweetly, then explained, deliberately dumbing down her language again, "Ain't ah knowin' what yer thinkin' here, *cher*? You, a Southerner-turned-Yankee raise yer precious nose at mah croup syrup. Like all doctors, ya think folk healers are quacks."

"Don't presume to guess what I'm thinking, *chère*. Just because I said your concoction stinks, doesn't mean I disapprove of your work; so, no need to pitch a hissy fit." He inhaled and exhaled, as if to control his temper, then said in a softer tone, "You have to admit, there are lots of charlatans out there, putting out magic elixirs that cure everything from constipation to cancer, but—"

She put up two hands to halt his words. "Truce," she declared with a laugh. "Anyways, how come it's taken you so long to get through medical school? You gotta be at least thirty."

"Thirty-one," he said. "I spent three years in the Army during the war as a combat medic."

Ah, Louise realized the irony then. Her Phillipe had intended to study medicine after the war, as well. Unfortunately, he hadn't survived to fulfill that dream. It wasn't a subject she wanted to discuss further. And she didn't have to because, just then, a whimper came from within the cottage, followed by the sound of tiny feet walking through the rooms. "Tante Lulu!" Adèle cried, dragging her pet blanket on the floor behind her.

Louise opened the door and lifted the child into her arms, blanket and all.

"Lulu?" Justin inquired.

"This is Adèle," she said, kissing the top of the girl's

tousled hair. "From the time she was a toddler, she was unable to say Louise, so, Lulu it became. And stuck."

Justin nodded but said nothing, studying the two of them. With Adèle's cheek pressed against hers, staring at the stranger, Louise knew there was a strong resemblance, which she didn't bother to explain.

And what he thought was obvious. Louise could almost see the facts click in his bachelor head. *Young bayou woman. Not so attractive. A little bit snippy. Has a child. Not for me!*

Not that Louise cared.

Much.

But she was annoyed.

Very annoyed.

And something shifted inside of her, something important which she would examine later.

Uh-oh! the voice in her head said, immediately followed by, "It's about time!" as if Jude were speaking to someone up above.

When Adèle went inside to get one of her dolls, Louise and Justin carried the produce boxes and the flowers to his truck. "See you around," Justin said just before lifting himself up to the driver's seat of his truck. Then he did the worst thing possible. He winked at her.

To Louise, it was the most patronizing, condescending gesture, when done without any evidence of attraction on his part. Like the most popular boy in school winking at the shy, fat wallflower.

A pity wink.

How pathetic! Louise practically growled at what was tantamount to waving the red flag before a bull. A challenge if she ever saw one. How dare he make her feel pathetic?

In that moment, Louise recalled that there was a time when she was the epitome of Cajun Sass, a bayou girl who could stand up to the most arrogant male, and there were plenty of them in bayou land. It had nothing to do with beauty, exactly. More with attitude, which translated to attractiveness, even sensuality. That young Louise never would have allowed Justin Boudreaux to treat her like she was less than what he was accustomed to.

The question was: How to regain her Cajun Sass when she'd lost it for five long years?

On the other hand, did a bayou-born gal ever lose her Cajun Sass?

Maybe she should check her mother and grandmother's receipt books to see if they'd written a recipe for Cajun Sass. Which was highly improbable.

Or was it?

She laughed out loud.

And heard laughter in her head, too.

CHAPTER 2

He wasn't Hank Williams, but, "Hey, good lookin'..."

t was a week later, on a hot Sunday afternoon, that Justin was back in Houma. He had his brother Leon to thank for his being at this boring-as-hell Crawfish Festival at Our Lady of the Bayou Church. They were leaning against a tupelo tree at one side of the front lawn, secretly sipping at cold cans of Dixie Beer, watching the crowd.

Justin didn't get that much time off from his residency at the hospital in New Orleans, and a Sunday afternoon spent watching old geezers play bingo and shrieking kids run around in organized games was not his idea of fun. Yeah, there was the wild zydeco music played by a local band. And the piles of spicy, boiled mudbugs, corn on the cob, boudin sausage, and potatoes being served on newspaper-covered tables were a sloppy delicacy he missed most when up in Cambridge.

But, really, Justin was beat, physically and emotionally. Doctoring did that to a person sometimes. "No offense,

Leon, but I'm gonna head back to my digs in Nawlins and take a nap." He shared an apartment in a Creole cottage on Lafayette Street with two interns from Charity Hospital. "I was up till two last night."

"With a hot date?" Leon asked hopefully.

"Hah! More like a breech birth of twin boys that didn't want to join their five sisters. Followed by a stabbing of a sixteen-year-old kid who bled out. And a massive heart-attack victim who survived but is on a breathing machine today." Justin had no interest in obstetrics as a profession, but he had to admit to a great satisfaction in bringing forth new life. The teenager with a pierced lung had been a goner before they even examined him, but still a soul-rending loss. It had taken Justin and the doctor on emergency duty an hour to stabilize the obese, chain-smoking heart-attack victim, who hopefully had been scared into a change of lifestyle.

"Ah, my brother, the doc-tor!" Leon teased. "Betcha women crawl all over yer sexy self. Betcha mamas are linin' up to introduce their daughters to a handsome Cajun who'll have a money tree in the back yard when he opens his practice. Betcha those Yankee chicks go ga-ga over yer southern accent."

Justin elbowed his brother and looked left and right to show there were no women lining up. "In truth, I can't recall the last time I had my ashes hauled. As for a money tree...me, I don't have two greenbacks to rub together, and it'll be years before I get out of debt."

"What about all those scholarships?"

"My scholarships don't pay half of my bills."

Leon shrugged. "You doan see me drivin' no Cadillac, either."

"As for my southern accent, Yankees call that redneck English."

"Poor you!"

They grinned at each other. "You don't do so bad, especially with the dames. Where's Lily Rose anyhow?"

Lily Rose Fortier was Leon's fiancée, and she was a stunner by any standard, North or South. A pageant princess from a young age, she'd recently graduated from beauty school and was about to open a little shop in the annex to Boudreaux's General Store, right next to the live bait ice box and the motor oil rack. Justin was the only one who saw anything odd, or amusing, about that juxtaposition. Everyone else thought it was perfectly normal. One thing was for sure, Leon didn't know whether to check his watch or scratch his ass when Lily Rose was around. If that was love, Justin wasn't interested.

Maybe Justin had been up north too long, as more than one person had pointed out. Despite Lily Rose's obvious physical assets, she held no attraction for a man who liked his women a little more intelligent. If that girl had an idea, it would die of loneliness. *Which is mean*, Justin immediately chastised himself. It was just that five minutes in Lily Rose's company, and his eyes started to roll back in his head at the talk of make-up, giggling, the latest fashions, giggling, and who was cheating on whom. Not that his opinion mattered. Lily Rose and Leon were scheduled to get hitched at the end of the month, before Justin returned to Massachusetts for graduation and to get his medical license.

"There she is now," Leon said, pointing toward the parking lot, then giving a wave to show where they were standing.

The first thing Justin noticed wasn't Lily Rose, even though she stood out in the crowd in a one-piece, white shorts outfit that left about a mile of her tanned legs exposed, a scooped neckline that drew attention to an impressive bosom, a red belt that accentuated her waist, and golden blonde hair that had been teased high and full in that Southern Belle tradition, the higher the hair, the closer to heaven. No, what struck Justin was that Lily Rose was traveling with a posse of two similarly dressed slick chicks, both of them smiling his way, giggling, and he knew he'd been set up.

"You didn't!" he accused his brother. "Since when do you play Cupid?"

Leon waggled his eyebrows, unrepentant. "Those ashes are piling up."

"Pfff!" But then, Justin exclaimed, "Hubba hubba!" and he wasn't remarking on Lily Rose or her whistle-bait friends. No, it was a new arrival on the scene. Walking out of the church activity center was a woman in a knee-length, haltered sundress, white polka dots on a red background. A petite but sensational figure was outlined by the fitted bodice that flared out from the waist over curvy hips. Long, dark brown, almost black hair hung in waves about her bare shoulders. Even from this distance, he could see that red lipstick matched the red in her dress, drawing the eye like an erotic magnet.

And he wasn't the only one caught by her allure. As she walked down the steps, a man going up did a double take, and smiled.

Louise didn't smile back, if she even noticed the attention.

"*Mon Dieu!* Who…is…that?" Justin asked.

"Who…oh…that's Louise Rivard. Lulu," his brother said, finishing his beer and tossing the can into a waste receptacle.

"No. No, no, no!" Justin declared, shaking his head emphatically. He got rid of his beer can, too. "I've met Louise, and that is not her."

"She's let herself go lately," Leon admitted, "but this is the way she used to look before her Big Grief. In fact, I remember her decked out in that very dress, cutting a rug at the USO in Nawleans during the war."

"Big Grief?" Justin had to laugh. Sometimes he forgot the way Southerners came up with such wacky concepts for every little thing. The War of Northern Aggression (referring to the Civil War), the Big Lazies, Blue Devils, Hissy Fits, and his grandmother's old standby excuse for why bayou women behaved the way they did, Cajun Sass.

One time he'd asked gran'mère how come girls got to blame all their bad deeds on Cajun Sass, and she'd told him it was because they needed that defense against the Cajun Brass of bayou bad boys. He hadn't understood what she'd meant at the time. He did now.

"Yep. Lost her fiancé in the war and been wallowin' in her mourning ever since then."

"Kind of selfish of her, considering her having a bun in the oven back then. A child needs a mother's undivided attention." Justin did volunteer work in a low-income clinic in Boston where he saw numerous examples of neglected children...the war babies delivered to women too young and unprepared for motherhood, many of them illegitimate and unwanted.

"Oh, that's not her child. It's her niece. And she gives the girl plenty of attention," Leon continued. "Too much, maybe. Nothin' selfish there."

Justin frowned, trying to recall if Louise had introduced the little girl that way, or if he'd just assumed. Yeah, now that he thought about it, the child had called her tante, or aunt. Tante Lulu. A dumb mistake. But, more than that, his assumptions about her appearance bothered him the most. He wasn't usually so blind. As a doctor, he was trained to see beyond the obvious.

Even worse, he suspected that he'd been a mite rude. He might have shown his lack of interest in her, single man to single woman, in some inadvertent, but insulting way. Not to mention his questioning the validity of herbal medicine. What an opinionated ass he must have appeared.

Seeing Justin's interest, Leon advised, "Forget about lookin' Louise's way, brother. You have as much chance with her as a one-legged man in an ass-kicking contest. Better men have been shot down."

Justin arched his brows at what he considered a challenge. "See you later," he said and walked away from his brother.

"Whoa! Where you going?"

"To make amends." His mama always said you couldn't undo burnt roux, but Justin figured he could try to offer Louise a different dish, or rather a different version of himself, hopefully one a lot less opinionated.

"But…but aren't you going to wait for Lily Rose and her friends?"

"Nope." *Find some other sap to occupy your girlfriend's girlfriends.*

Louise didn't notice him at first because she'd walked over to the playing field where a children's game involving balloons and bushel baskets was in full swing. A waist-high, portable fence had been arranged around the perimeter of the designated area. Laughing and cheering before the fence, Louise's attention was focused on a dark-haired girl with pigtails, wearing a pink, ruffled blouse, pink dungarees, and pink sneakers. He could see why he'd mistakenly believed she was Louise's daughter. The resemblance was remarkable, but then there was the family connection, according to Leon.

He was several yards away when he observed that she was taller than he remembered. But then he realized she wore high-heeled, wedge-type sandals that probably gave her a few inches. Even so, he towered over her at a modest five-eleven.

She was a small package, as he'd imagined in those baggy overalls she'd had on last week, but what he hadn't imagined was the curves. Perfect breasts the size of halved baseballs, a tiny waist flaring out over rounded hips, and he was guessing an ass resembling an inverted heart, his favorite kind.

"Lou-ise, Lou-ise, Lou-ise," he chided. Somehow, he couldn't think of her by that silly nickname of Lulu when she looked like this.

Her head jerked to the side. Apparently, she hadn't been aware of his approach. But she recognized him immediately. He could tell by the flare of her nostrils. Yep, he'd offended her on their previous meeting.

Not to be thwarted, he bulldozed ahead. "Tsk, tsk, tsk. Hiding your light under a bushel basket ain't the Cajun way, *chère*. Glad I am to see you turn a new leaf." He gave her a deliberate, full-body appraisal. "Dare I hope I was responsible?"

It was the wrong thing to say, he grasped immediately.

But before he had a chance to backtrack, or apologize, she put a hand on one hip, cocked her head, and said, "Is there anything worse than a turkey who thinks it's a peacock?" Then she turned back to look at the children's game, dismissing him.

"Aw, c'mon, Louise, give me a break. You were looking like Farmer Jane after a day plowing the lower forty. Now…"

"Now?" she prodded.

"Now, you're Hedy Lamar's body double."

He caught a brief flash of a smile twitch at her luscious lips, which he could see now, up close, were a slick Kiss-me-please crimson, but she managed to hold the smile back. "Save the fake compliments, Casanova."

He made an X sign over his chest and said, "Cross my heart and hope to die. You are hotter than a goat's behind in a pepper patch."

She laughed out loud. "Such charm!"

"Oops. It was the best I could come up with on short notice. That's an expression my grandfather used when teasing my grandmother out of the grumpies. She would tell him he was as crude as a farting horse."

She gave him a quick survey that put him in the same farting horse category, but then conceded, "Sounds like they were a fun couple."

"They were." He reached over and took a strand of her hair between his thumb and forefinger, rubbing sensuously. "What did you do to your hair to make it so…" he wanted to say sexy, but figured it was too soon for that intimate word, "…luxurious."

"One of my grandmother's recipes. An herbal remedy."

He groaned inwardly, suspecting a trap. "Just don't tell me it has something in it like gator snot."

"I said herbs, lunkhead. Gator snot has its uses, but it's not an herb."

Gator snot has its uses, he repeated to himself, but had the good sense not to say it out loud. He put both hands up in surrender. "Truce?"

She shrugged. "That depends. Are you still dead set against folk healing?"

"I never said I was totally opposed…oh, maybe I did give that impression. But, darlin', I grew up on the bayou, too. I know the value of certain plants. I know that some modern medicines are just sugar-coated herbs I lived with in my backyard."

"Well, hallelujah! I do declare, an enlightened physician."

He gritted his teeth to keep from making a retort.

"And I have to make an admission, too. I want to throw up when I go into a drugstore and see something like Dr. Jessup's Miracle Herb Tonic that cures everything from baldness to toe fungus. In fact, I think it's on the shelf of your daddy's store."

"It is not!" he swore, but decided he should check next time he was there.

The whole time they talked, her eyes kept darting to the playing field, keeping an eye on her niece.

"I thought she was your daughter," he said.

"There you go, thinking again. Must put a strain on that Yankee education." She gave him a look, which pretty much said she knew how bachelors felt about single women with children. "But, frankly, she's the same as, for me."

In other words, if a guy wanted her, it was a bundle package. He wasn't thinking that far into the future. He couldn't, not with his career just starting off, and so unclear. But he was tempted. Very tempted.

"Can I come see you sometime?" he asked suddenly.

She arched her brows at him. "Why?"

"Because I'd like to get better acquainted."

"Why?"

"You're cruel."

She shook her head. "No. Just careful."

"Why?" he was the one asking now. "I'm not dangerous."

"Oh, yes, you are, *cher*. A dreamboat like you never hears no when he's hustling a woman."

Hustling? Hustling? "I hear plenty of no's," he contended, even though he hadn't done a whole lot of asking, or hustling, the last few years. Too busy with studies, and no money. But inside, he was patting himself on the back. *She thinks I'm a dreamboat. I'm practically "in like Flynn."*

"Listen. My mama allus said, beware of Cajun men. They have a twinkle in their naughty eyes. Sweet words flow lak honey from their fool tongues. And mischief simmers in their blood, sure as rain on laundry day."

He grinned. "As I recall, you accused me of turning Yankee last time we met."

"Oh, you Cajun, all right."

He loved the way she reverted to the language of their mutual roots on occasion. In fact, he suspected that she alternated between what Northerners considered an almost illiterate Southern language with words and sentences that clearly bespoke some education and intelligence. Did she do it deliberately? Probably. And it *would* fool outsiders. Not him. He could do Cajun with the best of them.

"Sugah, Ahm thinkin' y'all need a little *joie de vivre*."

"And you're the one to put that joy in my life?"

Her sarcasm was a little bit offensive. But he was undaunted. "I could try. What say we go out on a date Saturday night?"

She arched her brows in question. "Go where?"

She probably thought he was inviting himself to her house, to spend the evening on her porch swing, necking… or even petting.

Which was highly appealing. But even a dreamboat like himself knew that wasn't going to happen anytime soon. "There's a little club on Bourbon Street where we could dance and listen to music."

"You dance?"

He put a palm over his heart, as if wounded. "I'm Cajun," he said as if that said it all. It did. Cajun men were taught to dance from the time they were toddlers prancing around the living room, diapers drooping, in rowdy two-step dance moves to loud zydeco music on the family record player. He'd learned the words to "Jolie Blon" before he'd lost his baby teeth.

"I don't date," she said finally, and moved a few steps away from him, giving her attention back to the children's games.

He moved as well, closing the distance between them, so that they were almost elbow to elbow, hip to hip. Almost, but not quite. "Really? Dressed lak that? Thass a shame!" He was laying the Cajun patois on thick as bayou mud.

And she replied in kind with, "Mebbe I dress lak this for mahself, not to attract menfolks."

"Or mebbe you felt lak that in the past, but now you've turned over a new leaf. Mebbe you're ready to dip yer pretty toes in the dating waters again. Mebbe I would be a good experiment, to see if yer ready."

He thought she laughed, but she wasn't looking at him; so, he wasn't sure.

"Listen, Mister Almost-Doctor, I been dealing with men who look like you my entire life. Men so full of their own handsomeness they think the sun comes up to hear them crow. Frankly, a peacock is just a glorified turkey, in my opinion."

This wasn't the first time she'd made the turkey/peacock analogy in reference to him. "Wow!" he said. "That was brutal, but you've given me a bum rap, *chère*. Without really knowing me, you put me in a box, smacked a label on it, and set it on a shelf marked 'Toxic'."

She blushed, seeming to realize she might have gone a bit too far. "Maybe you're right. I do tend to jump to conclusions sometimes."

He was no fool. He took an opening any way he could get it. Besides, now this opinionated woman was a challenge. And, don't forget, she thought he was handsome as a peacock. He barely suppressed a smile as he said, "Okay, apology accepted," though she hadn't really apologized, "but how about me coming out to your place and you teach me about herbal medicines? You wouldn't deny a doctor his learning, would you?"

She turned to look at him then.

He fluttered his eyelashes at her.

She smiled and shook her head at his persistence. "Are you serious?"

"I am," he said, and he meant it, though getting to know Louise better would be an obvious lagniappe. Never let it be said there weren't two ways to skin a rabbit.

Any further discussion on the subject was halted by a sharp scream.

Both Justin and Louise's heads jerked forward toward the playing field where the games had ended abruptly.

Still screaming was Louise's niece Adèle who was bending over another little girl who was lying on the ground, unmoving. "She's dead! She's dead!"

Without hesitation, Justin leaped over the fence and ran as fast as he could. Louise wasn't far behind.

CHAPTER 3

Just one more chance to make a good impression...

ouise calmed Adèle down, but her daughter still hugged her tightly, with arms wrapped around her neck and her legs locked around her hips, as they both watched Justin. He was kneeling on the ground where he worked on the semi-conscious child, lying flat on her back. It was Anna Belle Gaudet, a friend of Adèle's.

Father Mark had offered to call for an ambulance, but since there were no full-time emergency teams nearby, it was deemed more expedient to get the child stabilized and take her to a medical facility themselves. In the meantime, Anna Belle's mother, Marie, arrived in a panic. *"Mon Dieu!* I just went inside to tinkle. I was only gone a minute. What happened?"

Marie hadn't been addressing anyone in particular, but it was Adèle who answered in a wail, "We was runnin', me 'n' Anna Belle, real fast, 'n' then she jist stopped and fell over, dead."

"Shh! She's not dead. She's just winded." Louise hoped.

Marie made a tsking sound before dropping down to her knees on the other side of her daughter and asked Justin, "Are you a doctor?"

He nodded, not bothering with the "almost a doctor" explanation.

"Anna Belle has the asthma. She isn't supposed to exert herself at all, 'specially not on a hot day like today."

Justin had been giving the little girl artificial respiration, alternating between breaths into her mouth and pumping his locked hands against her chest. Then, he put his ear to Anna Belle's chest and checked her pulse with fingertips to her neck, things he'd already done several times. "Her heart rate and pulse are steady now, but her breathing is still thready. Does she have a aerohalor? Or any medication she takes?"

"She has the inhaler. At home. No medicine. Jist herbs that Miz Rivard...Louise's mother...gave me a long time ago, to make a steam tent." Her voice was teary and guilt-ridden. "She was gettin' better this past year. I thought—"

"She's gonna be fine, Mrs. Gaudet," Justin told her. "Look, she's already starting to wake up."

Anna Belle's eyelids were fluttering. But she was wheezing, her chest moving visibly with each breath. Which even Louise knew was not normal and not a good sign. It didn't help that she was starting to sob, understandably frightened.

"Do you have a family doctor?"

"Well, Doctor Clovis, I s'pose."

Doctor Clovis LeDeux was eighty if he was a day, and a closet alcoholic, but still doing house calls when needed to his patients along the bayou. His office was located in the front library of his Greek Revival mansion on the outskirts of Houma.

Justin exchanged a look with Louise, which pretty

much said what he thought of medical care in his home region.

"But we haven't seen Doc Clovis fer a long time," Marie continued. "Like I said, Anna Belle's been so much better, and my family doctors ourselves, mostly."

Again, another meaningful look from Justin to Louise.

What? Is he blaming me for medical care in these remote regions? And there's nothin' wrong with home doctoring, for the most part. It's worked for a couple hundred years here on the bayou.

Louise set Adèle on her feet and asked Justin, "Is there anything I can do?"

He indicated with a movement of his eyes that she should get Marie out of the way so that he could pick up the child. "Can you go find my brother and tell him to bring his car up closer? Someone can call ahead to Dr. Clovis."

"We can use Lillian, my car. She's a jalopy, a 1940 Chevy Cabriolet, but the old girl runs," Louise said.

He nodded and she took Adèle's hand in hers. The two of them, along with Marie, ran toward the parking lot. Lots of people were standing around, watching, and some of them called out questions to her, but she just waved at them and said, "Later."

Adèle was asking lots of questions, too, but Louise assured her that this wasn't her fault and Anna Belle was going to be all right, but that, at the moment, the two of them had to be heroes to the rescue.

"Like my daddy?"

Louise had told Adèle that her father was a soldier who died to rescue a lot of people. She hadn't mentioned which soldier she meant, her fiancé or her brother, and thus far, Adèle hadn't wanted any more details. "Yes, sweetie."

"Good." Adèle beamed up at her.

Louise's heart clutched and tears misted her eyes. If only Phillipe had known his daughter, or had ever been aware of her existence, if only in the womb. He would have been so proud!

Somehow they managed to fit everyone in her car, Louise driving with Adèle in the passenger seat, and Justin and Marie in the back seat with a gasping Anna Belle lying across their laps. Justin had to give her artificial respiration again, two more times.

Dr. Clovis met them at the open front door of his house. The gin blossoms on his bulbous nose and his flushed cheeks were a testament to his decades-long love affair with booze. His breath smelled of the peppermint Lifesavers he must purchase by the bushel. Everyone on the bayou knew that the old man had a drinking problem, including his three ex-wives, but it never interfered with his work, as far as Louise knew.

Justin, who had to know the old man's history, looked at him with skepticism, probably through the lens of his almost-doctor glasses.

She elbowed him to keep his thoughts to himself.

With an oxygen mask and then a large inhaler in place, Anna Belle's breathing soon came back to normal. And she was not only conscious, but babbling in a steady stream of chatter to Adèle and anyone else who was in the vicinity about her adventure.

Two hours later, Louise was driving Justin back to the church grounds where he hoped that his brother would still be waiting for him. Otherwise, she would have to take him back to his father's store. He needed to make the evening bus to New Orleans in order to be on duty later that night. Adèle was asleep on the back seat, the chaotic day having caught up with her.

"I'm impressed," she told him.

"With Dr. Clovis?" he scoffed.

"No, you fool. Although he did a fine job, you must admit. No, I meant you."

"Why?"

"You acted in such a professional manner back at the festival."

"You mean, like a doctor?"

She slapped him on the arm at the sarcasm.

"Really, this chip on your shoulder about doctors is starting to irritate me, *chère*."

She just grinned.

Which further irritated him. "Exactly what has your knickers in a twist?"

She exhaled on a long sigh. "You had no need to badmouth folk healing."

"In my defense, there are quacks out there who—"

"Generalize much, my friend?"

He gritted his teeth. "Y'know, frogs have it easy. They just eat what bugs them."

"Are you saying you want to eat me?" she asked, then cringed, hoping he wouldn't get the inadvertent double entendre.

No chance! He was the one grinning now.

"No need for you to be grinnin' like a cabbage-eatin' skunk," she sniped.

"Sorry," he said. Not at all sorry, if that continuing grin was any indication. "You were saying that I acted in a professional manner. And...?"

"I meant that you didn't hesitate. Just stepped in. Were decisive. And competent."

"And that surprised you?"

"Well," she smiled his way. "I admit, I was predisposed to not like you."

"Because I behaved like an ass before."

She arched her brows at him. "A little bit."

"So, since you like me now—"

"I didn't say that," she interrupted him with a laugh.

"Since you *approve* of me now, does that mean I can come see you some time?"

"You are persistent."

"Nothing ventured, nothing gained." He waggled his eyebrows at her. "How about tomorrow afternoon?"

"I need to go out in the swamps to gather some herbs. My supplies are low."

"Swell," he said and trailed a fingertip lightly over her forearm, from elbow to wrist. The gesture might have been playful, but the expression in his dark Cajun eyes was hungry and lustful. Serious business, that.

The fine hairs stood out all over Louise's body, coming to erotic attention, and she had to wonder if she was making a big mistake, or marking an important turning point in her barren life. She had only this past week taken steps to get her Cajun Sass back, thanks to some tips in her mother's family herb journal. Maybe this was taking a giant step further in that direction when what she needed was baby steps.

"I feel as if I've opened the chicken coop door to a starving dog."

"I don't know about starving. Well, yes, you could say that." He smiled that devastating smile of his.

"You are way out of my league," she said before she had a chance to bite her tongue.

"If you don't want to run with the big dogs, darlin', you can always stay hidden under the porch."

That was a challenge if she ever heard one.

She lifted her chin and said, "Bow wow!" Then she winked at him. Where she got the nerve, she had no idea. Must be some hidden reservoir of Cajun Sass.

To her immense satisfaction, he visibly gulped.

~

When Cajun Sass meets Cajun Brass...

Louise woke the next morning to what looked to be a beautiful day, not too hot, not too humid.

After a quick visit to the bathroom and whispered morning prayers, including a hello to St. Jude, she padded out to the kitchen where she turned on the coffeepot. She also flicked the knob on the small radio on the counter, already set to the Cajun station which played traditional French bayou music and the more raucous zydeco accented by the occasional "E ha ha!" The music was mixed in with local news and weather reports. She'd been right. The temperature was expected to be a balmy eighty this afternoon.

Much attention was being given that day to the musician Harry Choates who'd died suddenly at the age of only twenty-eight. Poor boy! His song "Jole Blon" was hugely successful, and the radio commentators were predicting that he would be known later as the godfather of Cajun music.

She took a couple sips of coffee. Then, since it was Monday, she went to the little room off her bathroom and started the weekly laundry, a tradition in Cajun country, though a much bigger deal in the old days when the families were large and the loads numerous. Even with just her and Adèle, there was plenty of dirty clothing. Probably because Louise was a little bit fussy about keeping her child clean and well-dressed and above reproach, the worry of many single mothers, who always felt they were under the gossipy eye of neighbors. Not that anyone knew she was a mother, but still...

While her first load was running, she went back to the kitchen and started a pot of red beans. She sautéed the Cajun Holy Trinity...onions, bell peppers, and celery...in some leftover bacon fat from the jar she kept in the ice box, followed by thin slices of andouille sausage. To that, she added the dry beans she'd been soaking overnight and covered the batch with water, bringing it to a boil, then lowered it to a soft simmer. It would cook the entire day and be served with rice and corn bread. Tabasco sauce would give the dish some spice.

Monday red beans and rice—another Cajun tradition from the past when women would work laundering, hanging clothes out to dry, then folding and sometimes sprinkling water on some items for ironing the next day. There had been no time for any special cooking on Mondays. Thus, the red beans and rice, which required no work.

It was funny, Louise mused, how she had come to embrace all the old Cajun ways. There had been a time just after high school graduation that she couldn't wait to get away from the bayou and all its old-fashioned ways. She'd headed to the big city of New Orleans where she'd been happy working as a typist at the Higgins factory, makers of the famous Liberty Ships. And, yes, she'd been a bit wild, living the principle of *joie de vivre* to the fullest, a frequent visitor to the city's USO, dancing and flirting with the soldiers.

And then she'd met Phillipe.

She sighed. Everything came back to Phillipe and that time in her life.

Her new wall phone rang, and she rushed to answer it before the noise awakened Adèle. It was Marie Gaudet.

"Sorry to call so early, but I reckon you're out and

about by the time the rooster crows. I wanted to catch you before you went out."

"How is Anna Belle today?" Louise asked as she gave the beans a quick stir with a wooden spoon, the phone cradled at her neck.

"Wonderful! The little imp. I do declare, you'd never know she scared us to death yesterday."

"Young'uns have a knack for springing back."

"I was wonderin' if you could send Adèle over fer a play date with Anna Belle t'day. It would be jist the thing to make everything appear normal again. I doan wanna treat Anna Belle lak an invalid."

"I s'pose so," Louise said, though she had been thinking of using her daughter as a buffer between herself and the too-tempting Doctor Boudreaux, assuming he came this afternoon as planned for her swamp foraging trip.

She wasn't exactly sure why she'd agreed to have him accompany her, especially when she knew what he was interested in. And it wasn't swamp plants. Ever since she'd tarted herself up with Cajun Sass after Justin's last visit, men had been giving her a second, third, even fourth look. It happened at the farmers' market. It happened while delivering medicines to her customers, even ninety-year-old Rufus Benoit, who'd pinched her behind and said, "Ah couldn't help mahself." It even happened in the toilet paper aisle at the A & P. Worst of all was church where she'd noticed two of the ushers staring at her and whispering lasciviously.

The thing is, Cajun Sass was about more than physical appearance. In fact, that was the least important aspect. There were many times, like now, when Louise missed her mother and grandmother whose wisdom would have helped her so much. In a way, they'd leaned in from beyond the grave and helped her anyhow. Proof was that

Louise had found all the information she needed on the subject, not in the always-reliable herb diaries but in some old letters exchanged between her mother and one of her sisters during World War I. Yes, the first big war, not the second one. Mixed in among all the news and gossip, there were paragraphs here and there about Cajun Sass.

Aunt Cecile had been complaining about life on a cold, cold army base up north where Uncle Victor had been grumpy and not paying any attention to her anymore…in the bedroom. Was it the chilly Yankee atmosphere that had cooled his ardor? Or something else?

Cici, you allus was the fool where Vic was concerned. Jist 'cause yer up in Yankee land doan mean you gotta lose yer Cajun Sass. And you know what that means. Style, Attitude, Smarts, Stubbornness.

Mon Dieu! *I fergot about the Cajun Sass. Style, didja say? Best I buy mahself one of them see-through nighties. Do you still have that Frederick's of Hollywood catalog?*

Her mother had reacted with: *Pff! Clothes is only a small part of the Cajun Sass recipe. Yer smart as a hooty owl, Cici, and stubborn as a cross-eyed mule. But remember what gran'mère usta say. It's all about the attitude. Walk with yer shoulders back and yer bosoms forward. Toss yer hair over yer shoulders. Smile even if yer fightin' the blue devils. Be proud, no matter if yer walkin' barefoot down the street or sittin' on yer threadbare davenport. Doan matter if yer poor as a church mouse or plain as a bucket. Pretend ya doan care what anyone thinks. An' they'll think, ooh la la, guar-an-teed.*

Louise smiled. She could almost hear her mother's words of wisdom with their deep southern accents.

Back to her telephone conversation, Louise told Marie, "I'll bring Adèle over later this morning, if that's all right with you."

"Much obliged. Do ya have any of that tea fer cramps?

I'm about ta get my monthly, and my belly is painin' me somethin' awful."

"Sure." Louise made a chamomile-peppermint mix that eased the cramps better than any drugstore medicine she'd ever tried. It was one of her most popular products. "I also got something new fer the bloat."

Once she had Adèle settled at the kitchen table with her usual breakfast of coush-coush—fried cornmeal mush with raisins, milk, and cane syrup—along with her Silly Friends coloring book and crayons, Louise went in to dress for the day. Reverting back to her Cajun Sass thoughts before the phone had rung, Louise decided that she wasn't going to make any special effort to attract Justin. It would appear too obvious. Bib overalls, like she'd had on before, tucked into calf-high rubber boots, worn over a long-sleeved undershirt, all to protect as much skin as possible from the swamp elements and animals, including the sun and insects, the pudding-like mud, and snakes, thorny bushes, and aggressive gators during mating season. She did take extra care with her hair, though, pulling it off her face into a high ponytail, but leaving some curly strands to frame her face. And she did add a belt, which really hadn't been necessary, though it made her waist appear unusually small.

That little smudge of tinted anti-chapping balm on her lips made her mouth look luscious, but that was an unintended side effect. It wasn't because she was trying to appeal to Justin. Okay, maybe she did want to show him what he was missing, but that was only a small part of her reasoning. At least, that's what she told herself.

When Justin arrived around noon, Louise was laying out supplies on the kitchen table. At his knock on the back door, she called out, "Come in, come in. The door, she's open." After entering the cottage's living room, he unapologetically began checking everything out ...the pictures on an end table, an open children's picture book on an overstuffed easy chair, a toy box overflowing with dolls and games. Her mother's basket of yarns. A stack of records atop an RCA console phonograph.

Like her, he was dressed appropriately for the bayou, wearing khaki pants and leather boots, a long-sleeved, faded blue button-down shirt open over a white under-shirt, and the same straw hat as before. He'd obviously shaved that morning, showing off a deep tan, the result of his summer in the South, she surmised. No doubt he was pale as a Yankee when back in the North.

"*Bonjour*, Louise," he said, coming forward and leaning down to kiss her cheek.

In that brief second of closeness, she got a whiff of the slightly medicinal carbolic acid in the Lifebuoy soap he must have bathed in, softened by the delicious tones of his Aqua Velva aftershave. Neither were overpowering. Rather pleasant.

Suddenly, she felt like a breathless virginal girl of sixteen, instead of an experienced almost-twenty-six. And she did not like it. At all! The skittering of her senses put her at a disadvantage, she decided, as if this were a contest of some sort.

"Bonjour Justin. *Ça va?*" she greeted him, forcing a casualness to her voice. She forced herself to not step back from his closeness.

"*Ça va très bien*," he replied, "especially since I'm here."

She arched her brows at him.

"I'm looking forward to our day together..." he paused and added, "...foraging." His attention was caught then by the items she'd laid out on her Formica and chrome table, a pretty oval style with a red top matching the seats of the red vinyl seats and backs of the the four chrome chairs.

The dinette set had been a proud purchase of hers two years ago when she'd gotten a belated life-insurance check from the government on her fiancé Phillipe. "Wow," he commented. "You are really organized."

His eyes took in the large canvas carry bag she'd made with special pockets for certain things, like the packets for plants and seeds, small jars and bottles, a pen and gummed labels, a hand spade, secateurs and a sharp knife, her homemade bug repellant, a machete, and a pistol. But then, he said, "Whoa! What are these for?" He was pointing to the last two items.

"The machete is needed for those places where the weeds are high. You never know when some snakes might be lurking about. Same is true of the pistol. I'm too small to wrestle an alligator."

He didn't laugh at her weak attempt at humor. "Do you know how to use a weapon?"

She nodded. "I do. It belonged to my brother Frank, and he taught me when I was scarcely a teenager."

"Have you ever had to use it?"

She gave him a look which pretty much said, "Are you kidding me?" Then she laughed. "It also comes in handy to ward off randy men who come a-callin' with naughty intentions."

"Point taken," he said with a grin. "I recall you telling me before that all Cajun men have a twinkle in their eyes… a naughty twinkle."

"I said that?"

"You did. I believe it was when you mentioned my being a dreamboat." He waggled his eyebrows at her.

She bit her bottom lip to prevent herself from smiling. Justin was way too charming. And full of himself.

"Speaking of your brother Frank, where's his little girl?" he asked then.

Louise felt her face heat with color. She wasn't ashamed of being Adèle's mother, but it wasn't something she shared with many people either. In fact, now that her mother was gone, and an old parish priest they'd confided in had been transferred, almost no one knew. "Adèle is playing with Anna Belle today."

"Ah. So Anna Belle has recovered?"

"Totally. As I told you before, you did a good job with her."

"Another compliment?" He bowed his thanks at her.

She cringed. "I haven't been that bad, have I?"

"*Mais oui!* You *have been* hard on me. I must admit, though, that it has been well-deserved."

"Meaning that you have naughty intentions?"

He laughed.

"So, we're even?"

"Well, you may need to offer me a little extra incentive...to heal my wounded pride."

"Hah! Your pride could take a few notches down. I haven't met a man so biggity since I don't know when."

"Biggity?" He put a hand over his heart, as if wounded. "You think this..." he waved a hand between the two of them, "is about pride? Hah! When I'm around you, I get light-headed. My brain goes mushy. And I blurt out things I normally wouldn't say...leastways, not this early in a relationship."

She was stunned speechless, for a moment. "That is so much malarkey. And, just so we're clear, you and I don't have a relationship."

He just stared at her.

Unspoken before them was the word "yet."

"Anyhow, let's get this show on the road...uh, bayou," he said. "What exactly are we looking for today?"

She chastised herself silently for falling into the

charmer's sexy banter. Breathing in and out to calm herself down, she then explained, "There are three particular plants I need." She sat down at the table and flicked carefully through one of her grandmother's receipt books. The spine of the hard-backed book, the kind that had been used since the Civil War for small business accounts or rent tallies, was broken, and the stained, sepia-toned pages were mostly loose, the whole held together with a rubber band. "Burdock and dandelion and nettle, those I can find just by walking along the stream, but it's these other more rare ones that I have to resupply."

She showed him one page for lizard's tail with its accompanying pencil sketch. The handwritten instructions...which must have been written by her grandmother, or maybe her mother—it was difficult to tell the difference —said, "For poultice on wounds, mash boiled roots. Also, for baby cutting teeth, put roots in glass of water with elm shavings, change water every day, add to milk or mix in honey for flavor."

"Where did you get these?" He pointed to the books.

"My grandmother started them. Then my mother added to them. Now me."

"These are fantastic," he said. "They remind me of the Audubon sketches of birds here in Louisiana."

She shouldn't care that he approved, but she did. Darn it! "This is the other plant I'm looking for today." She turned to a later page in the first book. "The mamou, or coral bean plant." The drawing showed beautiful crimson flowers with red beans inside black pods. This particular sketch had been hand-colored. Although the colors were faded, they were still vivid enough to differentiate, in fact, more lovely because of the shadings. The directions said, *Boil seeds. Drink liquid 3 x day for newmoanya, colds, bron-keyeyetis.*

Justin scoffed at this one, whether for the misspellings or the cures, she wasn't sure, and didn't ask.

"I'd really like to get to a sweet gum tree I've visited in the past. You're probably aware that healing herbs sometimes make use of all parts of a plant—the roots, the stems, the bark, the twigs, the flowers—and each has a different purpose. One part can even be poisonous, while another is beneficial. And the time of year they're harvested can make a difference, too. Anyways, I use the sweet gum leaves for headaches." She paused and asked, "Am I boring you?"

"Not at all." He tapped one of the receipt books and remarked, "These are a treasure, you know. They probably belong in a museum or something."

"Pfff! Museum people don't care about anything lowdown like Cajuns."

"Someday they will," he predicted. "But I know what you mean. From the beginning, when the Acadians first fled France and Canada, they were considered a lower class, ignorant people. Little credit was given to the fact that they were survivors, willing to live in the swamps, do the grueling, dirty work of shrimping or trapping, eat foods no one else would touch, like possum or gator, and cook them in a simple style without fancy sauces, play music that to the more refined ear sounds raucous rather than melodic, and—"

She was laughing, which caused him to stop and blush.

"I do get carried away."

"I take it you've had to defend our culture up north."

"A time or two," he admitted.

Louise wrapped one of the books in oilcloth...the one that had the plants she was seeking today...to protect it against any dampness or accident while traveling in a pirogue through the bayou.

"I'm ready," she said when she was all packed up. "Are

you sure you want to spend your day off out on the bayou?"

"Well, I can think of a few things I'd rather do." He gave her a quick once-over and stepped closer.

She backed up and hit the counter. She wasn't dumb enough to ask what he meant. She knew. His arrogance was maddening...and unwarranted. At least, she didn't think she'd given him welcoming signals. "That's the only activity on the agenda."

"Not even a kiss?"

"No! Why would I kiss you?"

"To be friendly?"

"I don't know you well enough to be friends. Besides, I don't make a habit of kissing my friends."

"Because you like me, then."

"What makes you think that?"

"I can tell. Your cheeks are flushed."

He put a hand to the side of her face, and she felt an electric shock, accompanied by a dizzying current of heat that traveled to all her extremities. She hadn't felt this kind of instant arousal since Phillipe.

Before she had a chance to object to his touch, his hand moved lower, and his fingertips brushed her mouth. "Your lips are parted," he pointed out.

She would have been hugely embarrassed, except that his voice was whispery raw. He was equally affected.

"Sorry. That was a bit too much...too soon," he said, stepping back.

"I should say!" She put her hands to his chest, about to shove him away.

But he leaned in quickly, took her hands in his, and brushed her lips with his, soft as a butterfly, fast as a dragonfly. Then, just as quickly, he backed up, grabbed her carry bag, and said, "You gonna dawdle all day, *chère?*"

Louise was stunned speechless, but only for a moment. Time to tie a knot in this boy's tail. As she walked out the door in front of him, she put a little extra swing in her hips, knowing without looking back that his eyes were glued to her hiney. She was pretty sure she heard him murmur, *"Mon Dieu!"*

Yep, the rascal *should* be praying. She intended to show him what a bayou gal with Cajun Sass could do to an over-confident man, with or without Cajun Brass.

CHAPTER 4

Love is a burning fire, or is that lust?...

Justin was playing with fire. He knew, sure as sin...and, yes, sin was exactly what he had in mind...that he was treading too close to the inferno where Louise Rivard was concerned. That little swish of her hips was a challenge he found both tempting and dangerous.

His stay in Houma would end with his brother's wedding at the end of the month. When he returned north to complete his medical studies, he would no doubt stay there; the opportunities were so much greater. And he liked it there, dammit. Sure, he was bayou-born and Cajun to the bone, but he was sick of the blistering hot weather, the bothersome gnats and dangerous snakes, the violent storms, the ignorance of some of the people.

Bottom line: he had no business playing with a Cajun girl when they had no future. He needed to ignore the gauntlet she'd thrown down with that wicked roll of her hips, which caused the fabric of her overalls to tighten over a bottom that was...*yes, yes, yes!*...in the shape of an inverted heart, just as he'd suspected. And, yes, it had caused the fabric of his pants to tighten, too, over an important part of his body.

Futile or not, he was sooo tempted. And like men, North or South, he was thinking with an organ other than his brain.

It didn't help that Louise was on to him, and was playing him with an erotic expertise that surprised him. Not just the thing with her hips, either. She must have put something on her lips to make them extra luscious. And the way she looked at him through half-lidded eyes...Holy *sac-au-lait!* Heat curled in his stomach and skittered out to all his extremities, lodging between his legs, which was already standing at attention, with an embarrassing flare. Good thing she wasn't looking at him *there*.

He tried to be a gentleman. He really did. Was it fair for him to start something with Louise when there was a fairly good chance he wouldn't be around for the long haul? But then, there was just as much chance that he was the one who'd be scorched in this play with fire.

With a grin, he decided all was fair in love and all that. And Louise was not so young that she needed a handicap in this contest of wills. He suspected she was not an innocent, especially having had a fiancé during the war. At least, that's how he justified his upcoming all-out assault.

"Why are you smirking?" Louise asked as she dumped her canvas bag into the center of the pirogue which was beached up on her lawn that abutted the stream. She untied the mooring line attached to a nearby tree and shoved the vessel out onto the shallow water, holding onto the rope so it wouldn't drift away until they were inside.

"I do not smirk," he said, taking the long-handled

paddle she poked him with and stepping into the stern of the narrow canoe, then sitting on the seat at the back.

She jumped into the pirogue, just front of center with an expertise born of years of practice, and dropped the rope. Still standing, she spread her legs for balance and used a long pole to punt them out onto deeper water. The canoe wobbled from side to side at first before righting itself.

"Holy *shit!*" he exclaimed, grabbing onto the sides of the pirogue, before using his oar to guide them with steady strokes in the traditional J-pattern. "You could have warned me."

She eased down onto the front seat, setting her pole in brackets along the side, then looked back at him over her shoulder. She was grinning. "Sorry."

"Sorry don't make the gumbo boil," he muttered. One of his mother's old sayings. Damn! They hadn't even started their trek, and Louise was making him feel like a namby-pamby idiot, almost falling out of the pirogue, and channeling his mother, for heaven's sake! Was that her intention? Of course it was. Lure the city sucker into the swamp and make him look like a fool.

He narrowed his eyes at her back, and vowed to make her pay.

In a way he would enjoy.

"Are you smirking again?" she asked, without turning around.

"Just smilin', sugar," he lied.

They remained silent then. With him paddling, they streamed steadily eastward. The earlier balmy weather had turned blistering with humidity. Sweat streamed down his forehead and its saltiness stung his eyes. He blinked several times, then swiped at his eyes with the sleeve of his shirt, only then to be hit by a swarm of gnats.

He swore under his breath and blew outward so the little buggers wouldn't enter his mouth or nose.

"Here," Louise said, turning adeptly on her bench seat and handing a small jar back at him. "Smear on a little of my insect repellant. The no-see-ems hate its smell."

No-see-ems was the name given in the South to the tiny midges or biting gnats because they were able to pass through screen doors with ease. Justin wasn't sure if they had them in the North, too. He didn't recall ever being bothered by them.

Another plus for the North.

Not that he was keeping count.

Not consciously anyhow.

He set his paddle down and opened the jar, taking a sniff. "Pee-yew! I can see why the bugs don't like it," he said with a grimace of distaste. But when he slathered a few fingerfuls on his face, it worked. "Thanks," he offered begrudgingly. For some ridiculous reason, he was blaming her for the bugs, and the sweat. Probably because he wasn't usually required to go to so much trouble to seduce a female.

Am I trying to seduce Louise?

Damn straight, I am.

Paddling and steering took all his concentration at first because of all the submerged or half-submerged trees, including the weed of the bayou, the loblolly, and the bell-shaped trunks of the bald cypresses with their roots jutting up out of the water here and there like knobby knees. Louise, who'd turned around again, called out directions, but it was still difficult to avoid the obstructions.

Just then, his focus was broken by a hiss and a loud roar, so loud he jumped on his seat and caused the pirogue to wobble again. It was a large gator, a female by its size; males could be up to twenty feet. Not that this creature wasn't formidable at about ten feet long. The gator was guarding its nest...a huge mud mound three feet high and ten feet across made up of decaying vegetation and twigs which held its eggs, as many as fifty or so. They'd just rounded a bend in the stream, and the nesting spot hadn't been visible to him right away. Otherwise, he would have stayed on the other side of the bayou stream. Which he immediately did, with him paddling and Louise standing and facing forward again, poling them forward.

"You knew that was there," he accused.

"Well..." she said.

We could have gotten killed."

"I would have saved you."

"Hah!"

The gator followed after them for a distance, showing off a mouthful of piano-key teeth, roaring a message which was probably something like, "Humans...yum! Taste just like chicken."

Louise sat down again and faced his way, with her back to the front of the boat. Some people couldn't stand that backward position and got motion sickness. Apparently, it didn't bother his over-confident Louise. She was, incidentally, laughing her pretty ass off. At him, no doubt.

"You know, I remember when I was a kid, we would try to steal some eggs from the gator nests. Don't have any idea what we would have done with them if we'd succeeded. Never heard of anyone eating scrambled gator eggs."

"Dumb," she remarked.

"You're telling me! Louie Mouton almost lost a leg one time when he tripped over a stump as we were running away."

"Like I said, dumb."

"Just for the record, Lou wrestled alligators for a living

for a few years until he ran for the state senate." He swatted at another swarm of gnats that surrounded him as he continued to paddle, first on one side, then the other. Then he got swatted across his face by a low-hanging swath of moss hanging from of a live oak tree. "I forgot why I hate the bayou."

"You hate the bayou?" she asked, obviously shocked. Or was it disappointed? Or both?

"I love it, and I hate it."

She made a snorting sound. "Make up yer mind, *cher*. You cain't speak out of both sides of yer mouth."

Speaking of mouths, Louise had one smart mouth on her, which was beginning to irritate him. He wondered if she was worth the effort. He gave her a quick survey and decided that, yes, she was. But she was going to pay for all this aggravation. Eventually.

"I'm bayou born, same as you, *chère*," he said, putting extra emphasis on the Cajun word for dear or darling, just to show he wasn't a total traitor to his roots. "But I've traveled more, seen other places," he tried to explain.

She made another snorting sound, which really annoyed him.

He went on anyhow. "I love the beauty of the bayous. The slow-moving water the color of fresh-brewed tea, which I know is the result of centuries of tannin seeping in from the bark of stream-side trees, but seem almost like some heavenly concoction." He cupped a handful of the translucent water and let it seep through his fingers. "The flowers are enormous and colorful, like one of those French paintings, too vivid to be real." He glanced to the right where a giant magnolia bush was covered with white flowers the size of lunch plates. "And their scents? Enough to draw a thousand bees. I know, I know, cornball to the max. And then there's Cajun cooking? Gumbo, jambalaya, beignets. My mouth waters just thinking about my mother's shrimp étouffée."

"But...?" she prodded.

"But I hate this blistering heat, and I hate gators and snakes, and I hate the slow pace of living here. Sometimes I just want to shout at my dad, or his customers, or the car in front of me on the highway, *'hurry the hell up!'* Oh, Louise, you have no idea how wonderful the change of seasons are up north. The summers are hot, occasionally, but never as uncomfortably steaming as it is here on the bayou, and when autumn comes with its crisp air and changing colors, it's well, a welcome change. I even like winter when a body just wants to stay inside snug before a cozy fire with snow coming down like goose feathers from the sky. The food is simpler. You have to try Maine lobsters with melted butter and Boston Cream Pie. Yum! The hospitals I've worked in are incredible, and—"

She put a hand up to halt further words and said, "It sounds pretty much like you've decided to live up north, for good."

Oh, hell! Had he ruined all his chances with her? "No, no, no," he disagreed. Honestly, he hadn't made that decision yet. "I'm just giving you a comparison, to show why I say I love *and* hate the bayou." No comment on how the scales were teetering. "Besides, I just thought of something else I like about bayou land."

"What's that?"

"You."

"What a load of hooey! You don't even know me."

"You wound me," he said.

She arched her brows with skepticism.

"A man doesn't need to know a woman to like her. First impressions count for a lot...maybe fifty percent of the chances for a connection to blossom."

"Is that some kind of northern statistical nonsense, or just a male line?"

He laughed. "Seriously, I knew the first time I saw you...I mean last week, not when you were a skinny little brat running around the bayou in your bare feet."

"You remember me from that long ago?"

"Well, a little. You were a lot younger than me."

"Anyway, you were probably in your bare feet, too."

"That's not important. Stop interrupting me. I knew when I saw you last week that there was some chemistry between us. And I wanted to see where we would go."

"That has nothing to do with liking me. It just means that you were attracted to me sexually, that you want to get me into your bed."

"There is that, but—"

"Besides, you weren't attracted to me when you first saw me last week, in my bib overalls. You only decided you would pursue me when I got my Cajun Sass on at the church festival."

She was probably right, but he wasn't about to admit that. In fact, he sensed a sort of destiny thing between. How cornball was that? "You're wearing bib overalls today, and I'm still attracted to you."

"That's because you now know what I'm hiding."

He shook his head at her bluntness and pretended to leer, as if he could see through her clothes, visualizing her naked body. But then he laughed and said, "You don't make it easy for a guy."

"If it was easy, it wouldn't be worthwhile."

"Let me ask you this. If you're so on to my devious ways, how come you're with me today?"

"Isn't it obvious?" she asked with a little smile. "I like you, too."

His silly heart skipped a beat at her words, or maybe it

was an organ down lower. But then, before he had a chance to react to her tantalizing words with something witty or provocative, she noticed a small island they were passing and she yelled, "Whoa, whoa. Turn around. This is where I found the lizard's tail plants a few months ago."

With some maneuvering on both their parts, they had the pirogue beached, then walked through the pudding-like mud on the banks up to a more grassy area. The island was no bigger than half a football field, he guessed...one of those bits of land in the bayou that were here today and gone tomorrow after a big storm.

He took the machete out of her carry bag and she picked up the garden shears. Together, they made their way through the thick growth toward the center of the island where there was a giant sweet gum tree. Dropping to her knees, Louise pulled from her carry bag a bunch of bags and dampened cheesecloths, as well as several tools. Handing him a knife and a jar, she said, "You can cut away some bark and scrape the sap into the jar." She was busy gathering star-shaped leaves which she put in one bag and the spike-ball seed pods in another.

While they worked, Louise instructed him. "It takes these trees twenty to thirty years to mature enough to produce fruit. And many of them get destroyed in storms before that time. That's why they're so rare in the wild."

"What do you use these things for?" He held up the jelly jar of sap he'd half-filled, and nodded toward the various bags she had arranged on the ground around her where she still knelt.

"Everything from the rheumatiz to diarrhea."

After she carefully placed each of her prizes in their designated pockets in the carry bag, they explored the rest of the little island. She found the lizard tail flowers, and he dug up the roots of several plants for her, one of which she claimed gave men a boost when their virility was on the wane. She waggled her eyebrows when she told him this, so, he wasn't sure if she was kidding or not.

"Are you inferring that I might need a lift?" He waved at his groin, just in case she didn't understand what he meant.

She did if the blush on her face was any indication. "Me, I would never make such an accusation about you." She batted her eyelashes at him in an exaggerated fashion. "Your swagger says it all."

"I do not swagger."

She shrugged, as if that was debatable.

He *grrr*-ed inwardly. "Just so you know, Louise, I am keeping a tally of all your digs at me. You will have some whopping bill to pay when this day is over."

"Really? And how do you expect me to pay for them? I'm just a poor bayou girl."

"Kisses," he replied.

She didn't respond to that. And her silence was telling to an experienced seducer like Justin.

Finally, she said, "Maybe I'm keeping a tally, too. Of all the times you come off as big-headed and snooty."

"I don't do that," he protested. *At least not knowingly.* "And how would you expect to collect from me? I'm just a poor almost-doctor."

She cast him a little Mona Lisa smile, the one as old as Eve.

And, like Adam, he was tempted.

For the next two hours, they paddled and poled along the murky waters of the swamp. Through its translucent depths, he saw catfish, the white crappies known as *sac-au-lait*, even an occasional grindle, the tough bottom feeder that liked the swamp mud—and wished he'd brought along some fishing gear.

Once they ran into a sheet of water hyacinths that

covered practically the breadth of the stream. As beautiful as it was, like a floating island of fragrant flowers, they were the bane of the bayou, having been introduced to Louisiana at the International Cotton Exposition in New Orleans in 1884. They choked other vegetation, cut off sunlight necessary for aquatic life, clogged waterways, and were in general a pain in the ass, almost impossible to destroy. Some frustrated farmers had even tried dynamite, to no avail.

They stopped here and there where Louise noticed particular plants that interested her. Goat weed, hackberry, Jesuit's tea, French mulberry. And the more fanciful names of Silver Drop, feverfew, tansy, horehound, and angelica. For each of them, she gave him a brief discourse on the benefits of the plant and its particular parts. He was impressed. Honestly, she could give a seminar on herbal remedies at his medical school and be praised for her expertise.

He noticed that when she spoke of her chosen profession…bayou *traiteur*…she used language peppered with educated terminology, but many other times she lapsed into the almost illiterate Cajun patois. Which he did as well, or at least he used to before moving north where he'd been subjected to so much laughter—and not the good kind. He heard way too many not-funny redneck inbreeding jokes about being married to his cousin, or a sister, for God's sake. Didn't matter that he had no sister. To his shame…okay, not too much shame…he'd been involved in more than one barroom brawl over that derision until he'd learned to just ignore the idiots. More likely, the mockery had lessened when he'd blended in by losing his accent.

Of course, Louise ruined the whole effect when she admitted, with a sly grin, that she also gathered herbs which Madame LeSeur packaged into mojo bags to be sold in her French Quarter voodoo shop,. Things like mugwort, bloodroot, skull cap, pennyroyal, and good old valerian, which has been around since the beginning of time.

He was shocked that she would unapologetically mix her folk healing with voodoo nonsense. "See, and you wonder why some people don't take your folk healing work seriously!"

"Don't get cross-legged over such a piddly matter," she advised him with a laugh. "The things I sell Sally LeSeur are harmless. And the tourists who buy them...well, they're dumb as dirt if they think a stinky bag hung by a string around their fool necks will help their peach pie win first place at the state fair, or prevent dandruff, or cause the town tart to suddenly fall in love with them. Talk about! Most of them are probably Yankees."

He laughed then, too.

Heat still shimmered over the bayou stream when they decided to call it a day in the mid-afternoon. The ride back to Louise's cottage was mostly quiet, but it was a deceptive calm. They saw a large water moccasin lying on the bank waiting for some easy prey, followed by the sudden flight of white egrets up up up out of the swamp. And gators were known to slide quietly with barely a splash into the waters, only their snouts and beady eyes visible. No wonder the early French settlers called it "sleeping waters."

He and Louise didn't say much, both of them exhausted. Not so much from their activity, but the intense heat had a way of draining a body of energy. He helped her beach the pirogue and tied the mooring line to a tree while she carried her bag of herbs and tools up to the house. He knew that she had to go pick up her niece soon.

"I had a great time today, Louise," he said, following her up to the porch. "Unfortunately, I need to hit the books. I have about five hours of study for my boards to get through yet today."

"I sympathize," she said.

"Maybe we can get together again some time before I return to Boston."

"Maybe," she replied, eyeing him warily.

What? Did she think he was going to jump her bones and take her right here on the back porch? Not that he wasn't tempted, even smelly and sweaty as they both were. They had to know each other a whole lot better for that kind of desperate gotta-have-you-*now* dirty sex.

On the other hand...

No, no, no! Timing is everything, and this is not the time. Yet.

But what about that fire in his belly? And lower?

Take a Tums, he advised himself. He was a doctor, or almost-doctor, after all. He had to smile at his inner humor. It was either laugh or cry of horniess. *Is horniess a legitimate malady? Sure feels like it.* "Okay. See you," he called out with a wave as he walked to his vehicle.

She was surprised...and probably a little disappointed, he hoped...that he didn't kiss her good-bye, not even a peck on the cheek. Especially with his comments throughout the day about the tally of kisses she was chalking up for her sarcasm.

She sighed.

Yep, she was disappointed.

But she was even more surprised when he showed up at her door later that evening. And hopefully the opposite of disappointed.

Now that is timing!

CHAPTER 5

Is sassy just another name for sexy?...

For a moment...a long moment, Louise stared after Justin, her heart heavy with longing, but not longing for him, per se. No, what she'd been thinking when he mentioned having to go back to his apartment to study and questioning whether he could see her again was, *This should have been Phillipe, who wanted to be a doctor, too. He would be at the same stage of his career. If he'd survived the war. Would we have been married while he went to medical school? Surely we wouldn't have waited. No, we couldn't have waited. There was a baby on the way. Oh, if only...*

She sighed. Again.

Justin had misinterpreted her sigh before he left. That's why he'd been optimistic enough to mention seeing her again. Not that he'd been specific about when she'd see him again. Darn him!

Should she? See him again, as in a real date?

She could think of a hundred reasons why that would be a bad idea.

And one which outweighed all the others. She wanted to be with him, pure and simple.

No, no, no! She made a concerted effort not to go down that path. Instead, she decided to go now and pick up Adèle, rather than wait until after she'd bathed and put away all the herbs she'd gathered that day. Louise had enjoyed a pleasant day on the bayou; let that be enough, she cautioned herself. She'd gathered some essential herbs. She was young and healthy with a life of hope in front of her. Optimism was sometimes a trait you had to work on, even when you felt just the opposite...*especially* when you felt the opposite. An added feature of Cajun Sass. Thus, she was smiling as she drove into Houma, singing along with the car radio which blasted out that new Hank Williams song, "Jambalaya."

All in all, it *had* been a good day. That thought kept running through her head. She wasn't ready to examine why, but for now, she felt as if she'd made a turning point in her grieving process for Phillipe. Was it due to her newfound Cajun Sass, or Justin Boudreaux, or just that old cliché about time healing? She wasn't sure. Maybe all three.

By nine p.m. that night, Louise was about ready to call it a day. She had the kitchen radio on low volume, playing some soft Cajun ballads from a new band, The Swamp Kickers, headlined by Kate Benoit. Most of the Cajun bands were male only because the dance halls where they often performed weren't considered suitable places for decent women. Pfff! Things like that were beginning to change since the war, but the process was slow. In any case, it was a refreshing change, hearing the traditional songs from a female viewpoint.

She was in her herb pantry, off the kitchen, putting away all the plants and seeds she'd gathered that day. Some were hung from the ceiling to dry out. Others were put in labeled jars. A few were put in hot water to steep, like a tea. Instead of warring with each other, the various scents melded together into one delicious aroma that said home and ancestry and bayou. The fragrance of comfort. Too bad she couldn't bottle it like a fine perfume or an air freshener.

She also wrote down what she'd found that day, and where, in one of the dozen black-and-white marbled notebooks she'd purchased at the Woolworth's five and dime after her mother died last year and she took over the business. She'd already filled four of the notebooks. It was important that she complete this recording of data as soon as possible, lest she forget the details if she waited too long. Which happened way too often.

Adèle had been asleep for the past hour, having been worn out from her day with her friend, even though their activities had been limited to indoor playing. After putting Adèle down, Louise had taken a leisurely bath with her favorite rose-scented bubble bath, also a Woolworth purchase. Despite the long day, some of it strenuous and outdoors under the hot sun, she wasn't tired. Her mind kept dwelling on her companion of the day...that blasted Justin Boudreaux.

Had she misread him totally? She could have sworn that his goal for the day had been to put the make on her. Instead, he hadn't even kissed her good-bye. Or made a specific date for the future. So much for his sexy banter through the day about her owing him kisses. Maybe his interest had been in learning about the healing arts, after all. Maybe her Cajun Sass wasn't as strong as she'd thought. Maybe the fact that she hadn't sassed herself up for the day had turned him off, like their first meeting.

Just then, there was a knock on her door, which caused her to jump. "What? Who would come calling at this time of night?" Must be it was an emergency with one of her customers...someone who needed a particular remedy real bad. That happened sometimes.

But it wasn't a needy patient.

It was a needy Justin.

Who was leaning against the doorjamb, obviously having recently bathed, if wet, slicked-back hair and a clean-shaven face was any indication. He wore a short-sleeved white T-shirt over khaki walking shorts and loafers with no socks. He had hairy legs which were oddly attractive.

Suddenly, a voice in her head...St. Jude, no doubt...said, *Beware, fair maiden, betimes the devil comes knocking on thy door.*

With all due respect...shut up, she replied.

"Who are you talking to?" Justin asked.

"St. Jude." She hadn't realized she'd spoken her thought aloud.

He smiled.

"Justin, what are you doing here?"

At first, he said nothing, just grinned lazily as he perused her body. Slowly. Head to bare toes. She wore a knee-length, sleeveless, pink cotton nightgown, her hair piled on top of her head into a loose knot. Her attire wasn't sheer, but still she folded her arms over her chest.

"Would you believe I happened to be driving by and saw your light on? No? Actually, I'm here because I owe you an explanation."

"For what?"

"The way I left."

She tilted her head in question, but she knew what he meant. How abruptly he'd left, with no kiss, and only a weak promise of another date. The very bone she'd been gnawing on.

"I was going to play hard to get…" he started.

"And…?"

"I decided that was ridiculous when I'm clearly easy to get. By you, anyhow."

"That is such a line."

"Nope. True." He made a cross over his chest. "Are you hard to get, Lou-ise?" he drawled.

"For you?" She made a scoffing sound at his outrageous banter. "Hard as a brick wall."

He ran a fingertip down her arm, from shoulder to wrist, raising the fine hairs in its wake. "Feels soft to me."

She slapped his hand away.

"Aren't you going to invite me in?"

She hesitated, then stepped aside to allow him to enter in front of her.

He leaned close as he passed her, sniffing. "You smell like roses," he said. "Have I mentioned how much I like roses?"

He didn't smell so bad either. Something piney and fresh.

"Seriously, Justin, what are you doing here?"

"Where's the niece?"

"Sleeping," she said before she had a chance to lie and say that Adèle was in her room, playing with dolls, and would be out any minute. In other words, a buffer.

He smiled and walked around the room, crouching down a bit to stare at the framed photograph of herself and Phillipe atop a bookcase, taken after Midnight Mass the last Christmas he was alive, picked up a knickknack of her mother's—a small china cat won in a penny toss game at a church festival many years ago—tapped the head on a little shrine to a statue of St. Jude—she had several around her cottage—and squeezed one of Adèle's stuffed animals, a long-tailed pussy cat. He smiled at the meow.

She could tell by his actions that he was nervous.

Just as she was.

For some reason, that gave her the impetus to open herself to him. "I'm as nervous as a hooker at Sunday Mass."

"Hah! I'm as nervous as a porcupine in a balloon factory," he contributed with a mischievous grin.

Her heart melted a little.

Sometimes, with all the grief and all the responsibilities she'd taken on the past five years, she felt old…like forty, or something…when in fact she was only twenty-six, almost. Young, really. But when was the last time she'd felt free? To be her youthful self? To be a little bit…wild?

And, yes, she was thinking about sex. She was no virgin. And she'd enjoyed sex with Phillipe. Why couldn't women be like men who dived right into affairs without examining all the what-ifs? Or without guilt…thank you very much, St. Jude. Some women did, obviously. And, Holy Crawfish! What was the sense of Cajun Sass if a gal had to be so rigid and uptight and protective of her virtue? Hah! *What virtue I had was lost in the French Quarter's Maison Rouge hotel to Phillipe Prudhomme five and a half years ago. Gladly.*

And truth to tell, Justin Boudreaux was the first man to really tempt her since then. Was it just a question of timing, like she was finally ready to move on? Or was it something more? An old saying of her mother's came to her all of a sudden: "Happiness sometimes sneaks in through a window you didn't know you'd left open." Yep, she'd left a window open all day today to let in the fresh air, but apparently she'd let in a lot more than she'd bargained for.

Justin sat down on her davenport, crossing his legs at the ankles and propping them on a hassock. Making himself at home. Way too comfortable, or pretending to be. He patted the cushion next to him.

Not a chance!

Well, maybe a chance.

"I thought you had to study tonight." She shifted from hip to hip, wondering what to do, wondering if she had the moxie.

"I did. I do. But I studied so much the words were starting to blur. Decided I need something to refresh my…" He waggled his eyebrows.

She shook her head at his foolishness. "How about a *refreshing* glass of sweet tea?"

He shrugged. "That would be my second choice, but sure."

She started to walk toward the kitchen, but then stopped and turned. She dropped her eyes before his steady gaze, but then raised her chin and told him, "I'm not a virgin, y'know."

It took him a second to realize what she was telling him and why. Quick as spit, he was on his feet. With several wide strides, he closed the distance between them and swung her into the circle of his arms, lifting her off her feet.

She dug her fingers into the strong sinews of his shoulders.

He buried his face in her neck and murmured against her ear, "Louise, Louise, you are precious."

She wrapped her legs around his hips for balance, which caused him to gasp and then stagger her up against the wall. She could feel his erection press firmly against her core, and a shiver went through her body. Now she was the one to gasp.

His left arm rested under her bottom, holding her up, and his right hand cupped her face. He gazed at her through half-closed eyes for a brief moment before he lowered his mouth to hers.

His kiss was surprisingly gentle at first as he learned her shape and taste, molding for a perfect fit, but then he glided his tongue along the seam of her lips, entreating her to open.

She complied.

His tongue slid into her mouth, filling her, then pulled back, slowly. Teasing.

She drew on his tongue, to halt his withdrawal. Teasing.

He made a low guttural sound in his throat

She smiled, even though their lips were still molded together. A smile kiss.

Sensing her silent laughter, he pinched her buttock.

She arched her head back and laughed.

He looked at her with a lazy smile. Then he came in again, this time with serious intent. His kisses hardened, demanding a response, insisting on her surrender but with an inventive, consummate skill that had her not only opening to him, but making her own demands.

He was obviously a man who loved kissing, not just as foreplay to better things, but as a goal itself. What woman could resist a man like that?

She was also a connoisseur of fine kissing, as taught by Phillipe. Not that she was thinking about Phillipe now. In truth, she wasn't thinking at all. Just feeling.

While his kisses went on and on, changing patterns, alternating between coaxing and ravishing, his hands were busy as well, caressing her back, cupping her bottom. Then he began slow thrusts and retreats of his tongue into the moist cavern of her mouth, emulating the undulation of his hips against her center.

She combed her hands into his hair, trying to hold him in place. She was being hit by so many sensations, above and below. Heat unfurled, and she didn't want to think or reason. She wanted all this and more.

His head shot up abruptly and through ragged breaths he gasped out, "Bed?"

She pointed to the hallway, and he walked them both, her still hugging his hips with her legs, to the open doorway. Once inside the small room with its single bed up against one wall and not much else, he pushed the door shut with his foot. Moonlight shone through the single window, but it was hard to see clearly. Not that she needed light. She knew her way around in the dark.

Justin stilled for a minute while they both listened for Adèle. Luckily, she didn't wake up. Which prompted Justin to toss her onto the bed and come down on top of her. More noise, but again, luckily, Adèle slept on.

He reached over and turned on the lamp on the bedside table, giving the room a soft glow. "I like to see what I'm doing," he said with a grin, kissed her quickly, then stood, staring down at her. There was lust in his eyes, and a bulge in his pants. Both pleased Louise, but she had a concern. "Justin? I can't take a chance that…"

"Shh!" He understood immediately and reached into his back pocket, pulling out his wallet, from which he took a flat metal tin marked Ramses which he tossed onto the bed beside her.

Protection. Good!

She opened her arms to him, but he shook his head. "Let me." He leaned down, and with her help lifting her body, he removed her nightgown. She was naked underneath.

"Oh, boy!" he murmured, then added with a rueful grin, glancing downward, "Down, boy!"

She felt kind of shy being bare naked while he was fully

clothed. "Your turn," she urged, waving a hand from his neck to his knees.

"Your wish is my command, sugar." He waggled his eyebrows at her and shucked down to his skivvies in no time flat, and then they were gone, too. He stood, hands on hips, legs spraddled, and asked, "Well?"

She stared, a bit bemused by his lack of shyness, and thought about repeating his comment of "Oh, boy!" but assessing the size of his erection, she smiled instead and said, "Oh, man!"

"I take that as a compliment," he said.

Under his continued scrutiny, she began to grow insecure. She had no idea what kind of women Justin was accustomed to, or even if he had a lot of experience, though his readiness with those prophylactics might be a clue. The bottom line, though, was that she knew her own shortcomings. She was not a voluptuous woman, and she wasn't tall and leggy—far from the Hollywood ideal of the perfect female body. Like that new actress Sophia Loren in *Quo Vadis*, who had legs up to her armpits and a bust that turned men into drooling baboons. Now that was va va voom! On the other hand, Phillipe had always said she had a hot-cha-cha hiney, the perfect shape and size to fill a man's hands. She'd forgotten about that supposed asset.

It was crazy how she had to continually remind herself that Cajun Sass was not about physical appearance, or not totally; so, instead of reaching for a sheet to cover herself, she extended her arms above her head, and raised one knee. A perfect pin-up pose, not unlike the one she'd done for a photo she had made for Phillipe one time. A going-away Christmas gift. Of course, she hadn't been nude then. Instead, she'd worn a red silk robe, but with a neckline so low you could see to the promised land, if a person were so inclined. Phillipe had been. And he'd made her recreate the pose in person. Several times.

Justin gasped and his you-know-what grew a little bit longer and wider, which she took for a sign of appreciation.

This is fun, Louise thought, liking the feeling of power she had. No, power wasn't quite the right word. More like control, like steering a car. You could go as fast or as slow as you wanted, or slam on the brakes, or press the accelerator to the floor and go all out wild and free.

"Why are you smiling like the cat that swallowed the cream? Are you hiding something?" Justin asked as he eased himself down onto the narrow bed, shoving her with his hip so that she was against the wall. Then he rolled on top of her and braced his elbows on either side of her head to ease his weight. He used his knees to spread her legs and settled himself dead center with his rigid penis aligned with her moist channel.

She was the one who gasped then, or swallowed a gasp, not wanting him to know how turned on she was so quickly. "Me?" she inquired then, in answer to his question, fluttering her eyelashes. "What would I have to hide, and where, with all my secrets exposed?"

He waggled his eyebrows back at her. "Not all your secrets, darlin'. I'm lookin' forward to discovering every single one of them, including the ones you don't know about your sweet self."

She felt a wave of excitement pass over her at his words. But, not to be outdone, she undulated her hips a few times, up and down, giving his no-doubt favorite organ a little slippery slide. "Was that a threat or a promise, *cher*?"

He took hold of her hips and held her firmly down on

the mattress. "*Mon Dieu*, Louise! Do you want to end this before it begins?"

"Me, I doan know what you mean." She fluttered her eyelashes some more.

"Vixen!" He pinched her buttock, then rubbed it in sweet, sensuous circles. "You'll be makin' me sing Hallelujah before the Gospel."

"Tsk-tsk! You shouldn't be making religious jokes during sex." She reached to the bedside table and turned over a framed picture of St. Jude.

He laughed. "How many of those things do you have?"

"Dozens," she replied.

"Are you serious?"

"I am. Because of how much St. Jude has done for me, I feel an obligation to pass out his relics and tokens of adoration to as many people as I can, without appearing to be a religious fanatic. I'll give you one before you leave."

"This is the weirdest conversation I've ever had with a woman in bed."

"I know, and we better stop talking about him now, or he'll appear in my head and nip this whole wild ride in the bud."

She could tell that he wanted to ask her about a saint talking in her head, or what she meant by a "wild ride," but he saved those questions for later, Thank God! Instead, he leaned down and whispered against her mouth, "I love kissing you."

"Good," she whispered back, "because I love your kisses." With that, she put her hands on both sides of his head and tugged him closer, kissing a line along his jaw, taking the lobe of one ear into her mouth and nipping it slightly, then putting the point of her tongue into his ear, stabbing several times till it was wet. Then she did the same to his other ear.

"Do you like that?" she asked, lifting his head to stare up at him.

"Are my eyes rolling back in my head?" he asked. "Of course I like that. Can't you tell?" He pressed himself tighter against her down below.

"Yep, you like it," she concluded saucily.

"Vixen!" he said again, then used the hair on his legs, which she'd noticed earlier, and the hair on his chest, to abrade her skin. Lightly. Teasingly. "Do you like that?" he repeated her question back at her.

Her moan was her only response.

"Now lie still and let me do my thing."

"Your thing?" She laughed. "You have a thing?"

"Shhh," he said and kissed her thoroughly, using his lips, and teeth, and tongue to turn her pliant and open. Then he moved his kisses to her cheeks and ears, paying her back in spades for what she'd done to him. Once she was mewling with pleasure, he kissed his way down her body. Down the center of her chest, bypassing her breasts, over her abdomen and belly, around her pubic hair, and down her thighs and calves. He even kissed the bottom of her feet, the inside of her wrists, and raised one leg, then the other, to kiss the back of her knees. By the time he returned to her mouth, she was writhing beneath him and whimpering.

"Now. I'm ready," she said, arching her hips up off the mattress.

He was obviously ready, too, but he pressed her downward, forestalling any more movement. "Not yet. I still have some secrets to explore."

"Oh, I don't know about—"

"Like your breasts. I wondered if the nipples would be tiny pink pebbles or rosy points when you were aroused," he said in a husky voice as he slid down her body to get a better look.

"And?"

"Both. Perfect, in fact," he said and took one of her breasts totally in his mouth, then released it slowly, like a suction, till he had her nipple and areola between his lips, then licked and fluttered the tip with his tongue till she'd reached the point of such intense pleasure that she felt like screaming but contented herself with a low keening wail. Then he did the same exercise on her other breast, and the thrumming bliss rose higher and higher, rippling out to all her extremities, then dead center between her legs where she shattered into what seemed like a million shards of pulsing sparks.

She'd had climaxes before. Of course she had, with Phillipe. But this was different. Maybe because it had been so long. Maybe it was his technique. In other circumstances, she might have felt guilty, as if her ecstasy was a betrayal to Phillipe. But now all she could do was pant and blink up at Justin with a dazed confusion.

"Do you have any idea what a turn-on it is to watch you come?"

How would I know that? she wanted to snap. In truth, she felt a little uncomfortable talking about it. Especially since he was equally aroused, as evidenced by his glazed eyes and parted lips and the continuing presence between her legs, but he hadn't climaxed yet. Reaching deep for nerve, she said, "Maybe I've been wanting to watch you, too." She hadn't given that a thought, but she would now.

He must have liked her saucy reply because his penis gave a little jerk.

"Now?" she asked tentatively.

He reached a hand down, parting her pubic hairs with

his fingertips, testing her moisture. "You might be almost ready," he concluded.

"Almost?" she choked out.

He smiled and used one finger only to find a certain spot in her lady parts, which he flicked several times before asking, "How does that feel?"

"Like there are a million butterflies down there wanting to escape."

He nodded as if satisfied with her answer and picked up the contraceptive tin, flicking it open with a thumb. With an ease that bespoke expertise, he rolled it on, raised himself slightly, and took himself in hand, easing his shaft inside her. Slowly. Inch by inch.

He blew out a ragged breath. "Oh, Louise! You feel like warm honey melting around me."

Louise was the one who worried that her eyes might be rolling back in her head then. Justin's entry and his words caused her to welcome him with the reflexive clasping and unclasping of her inner muscles until he was in her to the hilt. "You feel like silky marble. Holy crawfish! You... fill... me. So good!"

He rested his forehead against hers, panting, before he took her hands, encouraging her to caress his body. Then he raised himself on straightened arms and began the long strokes that her body had been missing for years, without her realizing what she'd been yearning for. The whole time, his eyes held hers.

It was true what they said about bicycles...and sex. Once you learned how, you never forgot. With that realization in mind, Louise entered into the "ride" with an enthusiasm that clearly surprised, but pleased Justin.

She rubbed her breasts against his chest hairs and purred at the delicious sensation.

As Justin watched her, his nostrils flared and he seemed

to grit his teeth to control his reaction. How like a man, needing to hold the reins.

She couldn't allow that. So, she deliberately clenched her inner muscles.

"Oh, my God!" he murmured and stopped moving on his inward thrust, causing his pubic bone to press against her pubic bone, and remained unmoving.

Huh! He can't stop now. She wrapped her legs around his hips, locking her ankles, and shimmied her body from left to right several times. She wasn't sure about him, but she about passed out at the extreme pleasure.

He made a sound that was a cross between a chortle and a choke. But he didn't move. Darn him!

He thinks I'm funny, does he? She bit his shoulder and soothed it with several licks of her tongue.

He laughed and said, "Okay, honey, you win. Hold on tight."

It was a wild ride then, but she did indeed hold on. And when she climaxed this time, he followed soon after with a roar of "Yeeeessss!"

At first he collapsed on top of her, the sound of his harsh breathing loud in her ear. But then he removed the condom and dropped it into a wastebasket by the bed, wiping himself with a tissue from the box on the bedside table. After that, he rolled over onto his side, tucking her under his arm with her face on his chest. The bed was too narrow for the two of them to lie side by side.

He kissed the top of her head and said, "You are amazing."

She kissed one of his flat male nipples and said, "You didn't do so bad yourself."

"I can't believe I lucked out like this," he told her. "When I came here tonight, the most I hoped for was a few kisses or maybe some making out."

"But you came prepared," she pointed out.

He shrugged. "As a doctor, I see way too many unwanted pregnancies. So, I'm always prepared."

"I need to go to the bathroom," she said then. "But, Justin, you can't stay the night." It wasn't just that she had a child, but his vehicle parked in the driveway would be like a neon sign announcing her promiscuity to any passersby.

"No problem," he agreed, understanding without her going into detail.

She relieved herself and washed her hands, noting in the mirror over the sink that her face was flushed and her hair, which had long escaped from its rubber band, was wild and bed-mussed.

What am I doing? she asked herself from the more sensible side of her brain.

Having fun, like other people my age, who are single. To fill a hole of loneliness in my life, the other side of her admittedly sex-hazy brain replied.

What about the future?

There is no future. Justin will be leaving in a few weeks.

So, sex without commitment?

Exactly. Why not? It works for men.

What about love?

Not a problem.

The sound in her head now was either a snicker or a snort, and she knew exactly where it came from. St. Jude had a habit of showing up at the most inconvenient times.

She brushed the tangle out as best she could and she put on the nightgown she'd brought with her from the bedroom, where it had been inside out and laying on the floor. Leaving the bathroom, she checked on Adèle, whom she could see clearly by the night light in the room, which she'd decorated in lavender, Adèle's favorite color, and white...all ruffles and lace. She picked up a teddy bear and placed it on the bed next to her daughter, who slept soundly, like she usually did. Leaning down, she pulled the light sheet over her little body and kissed her on the cheek.

When she returned to her bedroom, she saw that Justin, too, was sleeping sounding. Nude as a newborn babe, arm tossed over his head, his flaccid penis nestled between legs that were spread wide, taking up the whole mattress.

"Tsk-tsk!" she said. "Wake up, Justin."

Nothing, except for a snore.

She nudged his shoulder with her hand and said, louder, "Justin! You have to get up. Time to go home."

He opened one eye and peered up at her. Before she knew what he was about, he grabbed her arm and yanked her over and on top of him.

"You can't be here in the morning when Adèle wakes up," she told him as she tried to squirm out of his arms.

He held on tighter, his hands caressing her back from shoulder to buttocks. "You got dressed," he protested. "Not fair!"

She wasn't going to be diverted from what she'd been telling him. "Really, Justin, you can't stay overnight. Not just because of Adèle, but God forbid, your Boudreaux General Store truck is in the driveway when cars go by on the way to work. With the bayou grapevine, I'd be getting a dozen phone calls by noon asking if I'd got a nighttime delivery. They'd be calling me the bayou floozy. Talk about!"

"Floozy? And, actually, you could say I delivered."

She smacked him on the arm for his teasing.

"If you must know, I didn't drive the store truck. I borrowed my mother's car."

"You numbskull! Everyone recognizes your mother's red DeSoto."

"Guess I forgot in the heat of the moment." He laughed.

"It's not funny."

"Don't worry, honey. We have plenty of time till morning."

"For what?" she asked, as if she didn't know.

"More exploring," he said.

"Does that go both ways?"

"For sure, darlin'. I can't wait."

"I can tell," she said saucily, as she wiggled her hips over the newly blooming erection pressed up against her belly, evidence of his anticipation.

"Vixen," he said, leaning up to give her a quick kiss. "I must say, Louise, you are a total surprise to me."

"Oh?" She slid down his body to kneel between his legs where she raised the hem on her nightgown, pulling it over her head, then tossing it to the floor. "Is that surprise good or bad?"

He was busy, staring at her body for a moment, and she could tell that he liked what he saw, despite her earlier misgivings about her assets, or lack of them. "Definitely good," he said in a choked voice. Clearing his throat, he explained, "It's not that you come across as frigid, but you've got a hidden well of sensuality that doesn't show on the outside. You're like a special present on Christmas morning. As a kid, you are expecting another new shirt or a ballpoint pen, but instead you get a baseball mitt."

She laughed. "Me, a present?"

"Uh huh. You have a *joie de vivre* in the bed sheets."

"That's a new one," she said. "I think you're tryin' to say I've got some hidden sluttiness." She pretended to be offended, raising her chin.

"If that's sluttiness, then God bless sluttiness."

"Shhh. That sounds sacrilegious."

"What? You think St. Jude is gonna boink me on the

head with some celestial hammer, or strike me with thunder, or turn me into a leper, or something?"

She shook her head at his foolishness. "That's not funny."

"Besides, when I said God bless sluttiness, I meant that I am truly grateful. Sort of like a prayer of thanks."

"I'm not sure St. Jude would accept that explanation."

Fortunately St. Jude remained silent. At the moment.

The playful banter ended then when Justin said, "I have an idea."

And, whoo boy, was it humdinger of an idea!

CHAPTER 6

Begin the Beguine...

*J*ustin awakened just before dawn to the sound of birdsong coming from the open screened window. Lots of birdsong. That's the way it was on the bayou. Nothing ever occurred on a small scale. The swampland had every variety of flowers, trees, animals, snakes, and, yes, birds.

He smiled and looked over at Louise who was splatted out on the bed, face and belly down. He'd worn her out, in the best possible way. Three bouts of lovemaking; four, if you counted him going down on her.

What a shocker Louise had turned out to be. First, the transformation from Farmer Jane to Mother Earth to Mommy of the Year (or Aunt of the Year) to Hot Broad, and now Wild Lover. He wasn't sure what he'd expected, or even if he'd had expectations of landing in her bed, but her enthusiasm and lack of inhibitions were a welcome surprise. He couldn't wait to see what she did next.

Of course, this was only going to be a short-term affair.

Even Louise agreed about that. They'd discussed it in between one of their bouts of sex. She was still grieving for some long-dead fiancé, had a child to raise, and plans to build her folk-healing business here on the bayou. He was an ambitious almost-doctor whose future was uncertain, not just what his specialty would be, or if he'd specialize, but where he would do it. Besides, he was leaving for Massachusetts in less than a month.

Enough said. Everything was copacetic.

He eased himself off the bed, careful not to disturb Louise. He was about to draw the light sheet over her body, but first (*shoot me! I'm a man!*) he admired the view. She was short, but perfectly formed for her size. He was particularly attracted to her small waist, that delicious dip of her lower back, and her buttocks, of course, which were plump and nicely rounded.

Enough. He had to get going. Drawing on his clothes, quietly, he slipped out of the room, pulling the door half closed. After relieving himself in her small bathroom, he washed his hands and combed his hair. Opening the door, he almost ran into a little person standing there in yellow-and-white checked pajamas and a mop of dark hair, looking like a miniature version of her aunt. Justin wasn't particularly fond of kids, but this one was adorable.

"I hafta pee," she said, as if she wasn't at all afraid of the stranger in her house. But then, they had met on that day at the church festival when her friend had that breathing incident.

"Do you want me to wake your aunt?"

She shook her hair. "I kin do it myself." And she did. Pulling down her pajama bottoms and tiny blue panties, she hitched herself up on the toilet, did her business, wiped herself meticulously with exactly three sheets of toilet paper (she counted), and then washed and dried her hands. She'd been taught this bathroom routine well, apparently.

"Okay, are you going back to bed, or should I wake your aunt now?"

"Breakfast," she said decisively, already heading toward the kitchen.

Justin stood, undecided for a moment, glancing from Louise's bedroom to the kitchen and back again. In the end, he decided to let Louise sleep a little longer.

"My name is Justin," he told the little girl who was sitting at the kitchen table, waiting for service.

"I'm Adèle, but you kin call me Addie. I'm almos' five years old."

Am I supposed to give her my age, too? Or tell her to call me by some nickname, like Jus, or Justy, or Doc?

Nah, he decided, and instead asked her, "What do you want for breakfast, Addie?"

"Coush-coush."

"I'm afraid that's beyond my culinary abilities."

"Huh?"

He opened the fridge door, scanned the contents, and said, "How about bacon and scrambled eggs?"

She nodded vigorously.

While he was frying the bacon and scrambling the eggs and toasting five slices of bread, enough for all of them, in the event Louise got up soon, he carried on the most bizarre conversation. Adèle skittered from one subject to another, like popcorn on a hot griddle. Maybe this type of dialogue was normal for an almost-five-year-old, but it was beyond his experience.

"I like to color. Do you like to color?" she asked.

"I did when I was a kid, I suppose."

"We kin color after breakfas'."

Great! "That would be nice."

"Are you Tante Lulu's boyfriend?"

Hopefully. "Maybe."

"Boys like to kiss girls. Do you like to kiss girls?"

"Um, yeah."

"Blech! Miss Dawkins has big boobies."

"Who?"

"Miss Dawkins. She's gonna be my kindergarten teacher."

Please don't ask me if I like big boobies. "You said you were almost five years old. When's your birthday?"

"In this many days," she said, opening and closing her fists two times.

Twenty days, he translated. He would be gone by then.

"Boys have two-two's and girls have wee-wee's," she informed him, as if she were imparting some secret. "Do you have a two-two?"

"Um, breakfast is ready," he said, filling a plate with a little pile of golden eggs, a strip of bacon, and a piece of buttered toast, sliced diagonally. He had no idea if this was a sufficient amount for a kid.

"Thank you," she said politely. "Aren't you going to eat, too?"

"Yes, but first I have to go outside to do something. Stay put, short stuff."

She giggled at his name for her.

I really should wake Louise and leave, but I don't have to work until this afternoon, and, okay, I admit I'd like to continue the fun of last night. Yeah, a kid might hamper my efforts, but I'll take my chances.

Louise will probably kill me for sticking around.

Or maybe she'll want to continue the fun, too.

I can only hope.

With the decision made, he moved his mother's car to the end of her driveway and into her back yard so it wouldn't be visible from the road out front. He felt kind of silly doing it, like a teenager engaged in some illicit activity, but Louise would feel better, he was sure.

When he got back to the kitchen, he filled his own plate and sat down next to the little girl. The breakfast was good, if he did say so himself. And Adèle was eating up, too. He washed his down with coffee, which he'd made in the aluminum pot on the stove, and the kid got orange juice. Searching for a kid-appropriate subject, he commented, "So, what do you think about Snow White and those seven dwarves? Somethin' goin' on there, I bet." On the other hand, maybe that wasn't kid-appropriate. He shrugged dismissively.

Afterward, he cleared the dishes and Adèle went to get her coloring books and crayons. Louise was still not up, but then, it was only seven o'clock, and he had worn her out last night.

"Why are you smilin'?" Adèle asked, spreading two coloring books on the table and the box of crayons between them. "Doan forget to color inside the lines. I kin show you if you doan know how."

Thus, it was that when Louise finally awakened, he was saved from her tirade over his continued presence by the sight of him coloring Dumbo a pretty shade of lavender, Adèle's favorite color.

"You're still here," she said as if that wasn't obvious. What wasn't said, but she had to be thinking was "Why?"

"Addie woke up the same time as me, and she conned me into making breakfast, and then I had to color at least one picture, and I don't have to work until this afternoon, and..." He let his words trail off.

"Where's your car? I didn't see it in the driveway when I looked out. That's why I was surprised when I came in here and saw you sitting at my kitchen table."

"I parked the car in your back yard. Wasn't that smart of me?"

"What?" She rushed over and looked out the living room window. The big car was parked parallel to her back porch, filling a good portion of her lawn. "You ran over my St. Jude statue and the bed of impatiens around his shrine." Her jaw dropped at his nerve.

"Oops," he said. "Guess I miscalculated a little bit." *Good thing she doesn't know that I almost plowed her fig tree down.*

Adèle looked up at him and giggled. Apparently "oops" was an odd-sounding word. Then Adèle admonished her aunt when she returned to the kitchen. "Doan be mad at Justin, Tante Lulu. He's my friend."

"Oh, really?" Louise put her hands on her hips and frowned at him. She was wearing the sleeveless, pink nightgown she'd had on last night. It wasn't very revealing, but now that he knew what she hid underneath, well…

He stifled a grin, and said, with an exaggerated flutter of his eyelashes, "Are you hungry, darlin'?" In case she didn't get his double meaning, he added another, "I'll fix your *shrine* later."

~

When saints go falling down…

Louise was falling a little bit in love. Yes, it was too soon. And there was no future in it. But what woman wouldn't fall for a man who sat coloring a purple elephant with her child? Who cooked breakfast, for heaven's sake, and didn't consider it unmanly? Who made her bones melt and her inhibitions fly away with his lovemaking? She blushed to think of the things she'd done last night.

Justin went outside to move the car back to the driveway while she dressed Adèle in a violet top and white shorts with blue sneakers, forcing her to take the time to brush her hair and teeth before skittering off. The whole time the little girl babbled about something Justin had said or done. "Justin said milk makes the bones grow strong." "Justin's daddy has a store that sells candy. He's gonna get me some licorice whips." "Justin kin sing 'Old MacDonald' with all the voices real good, even the horse."

Once Louise had dressed herself in black pedal pushers and a sleeveless, stretchy pink top and white sandals, her hair pulled back into a simple ponytail, no make-up, she went out to discover Justin fixing the shrine with his little helper, the two of them chatting away like longtime pals. For some reason, she was surprised that Justin could deal so well with a child, sort of bring himself to child level. Maybe it was a skill taught in medical school. Adèle didn't usually take to strangers so easily.

"How's it going?" she asked, stepping onto the porch.

"Pretty good," Justin said. "Not much damage, except for a few toes that I can glue back on later after I get some waterproof adhesive."

The statue was about four feet tall and sat on a concrete slab. Jude wore a brown robe with a rope belt and his bare feet peeping out of the hem, minus three toes on his right foot. The blue eyes of the statue seemed to be staring at her in disapproval...for the damage or for her activity of the previous night, she wasn't sure. She would find out soon enough.

"We have to clean off Jude's hiney," Adèle told her.

"What?"

Justin grinned. "The statue fell backward into the mulch. We're going to hose it off."

"What're you going to do about the flowers?" There were crushed impatiens and spreading vinca vines everywhere.

"Dontcha be worryin' none, *chère*," Justin said. "Me and Adèle are gonna fix everything. Right, short stuff?"

Adèle beamed.

Oh, this is not good, Louise thought. This is just what she'd always avoided, letting her little girl get attached to some man who would eventually ride off into the sunset. It was one thing for her to settle for a short-term affair, but quite another to involve her daughter. She had obviously not thought this thing through.

But she had no time to ponder the situation now because her first client of the day had just shown up. It was Mrs. Benoit, the retired postmistress from Houma. She pulled her ancient roadster into the driveway beside the DeSoto, walked around to the back porch, and called out, as if his appearance were nothing remarkable, "Hey, Justin! How's yer mama?"

"Doin' poorly last night. Her feet get all swelled up when she's standin' in the store all day."

"She should soak 'em in Epsom Salts," Mrs. Benoit advised.

"That's just what she was doing."

"And how are you today, Adèle?"

"Jus' fine. Me and Justin are gonna hose off St. Jude's hiney."

Mrs. Benoit's jaw dropped but then she seemed to notice the tire tracks in the grass, the crushed flowers, and the tilted statue. "Looks lak someone had a little acci-dent," she remarked with a laugh.

She took Mrs. Benoit inside where they discussed the ongoing arthritic pain in her shoulder which had been aggravated by a recent bout of labor-intensive gardening. Louise prescribed willow bark tea for her, along with a salve that helped the swelling.

No sooner had Mrs. Benoit left than Clive Delacroix

showed up. "Whoa, Justin! What happened to ol' Jude there?" Clive also didn't seem surprised at Justin's presence. "I might have some paint samples back at the store to touch up those flaky spots."

Clive was the owner of a small hardware store down the bayou. You could find almost everything there for a home, from roofing tiles to turpentine.

"Thanks, Mister Delacroix. I'll stop by tomorrow and see what you got."

What? Justin is planning on coming back here tomorrow? To paint my statue?

After giving Clive some witch hazel salve for his hemorrhoids, she had a small break in which she prepared some lemonade for Justin and Adèle which she placed on a low porch table. They'd already set the statue straight on its concrete pedestal and removed all the damaged flowers and greenery. They were planting new ones which they'd transplanted from flower beds on the other side of the yard. It was actually looking better than it had before.

She was in the kitchen trying to decide what to make for lunch when Justin came in and went over to the sink to wash his hands. "I've gotta hit the road. I'll just have time to shower back at the apartment and make my shift at the hospital by two."

She nodded. "Where's Adèle?

"Went into her bedroom to get some paper dolls."

"That's what she does when she's overtired. She arranges all her dolls into families all over her floor to play with."

"Did I overtire her?" he asked with alarm. "I mean, she looked like she having fun, so, I—"

"No, no. She was having a ball."

He dried his hands on a towel and leaned back against

the counter, watching as she put some leftover gumbo and rice into several pots to warm up for lunch.

"Do you have time?" she asked, motioning toward the food.

"It looks good, but nope. No time." He still watched her, though. "You had a busy morning."

"I did, and actually it helped to have Adèle out of the way. So, thanks."

He nodded.

"I had four clients come here, and six phone calls," she told him. "That *is* a busy morning." It was obvious to her, and to him, that she was making conversation to fill the silence. The big elephant in the room was what had happened between them last night.

"Come here, Louise," he said, motioning with the fingertips of both hands for her to approach. He was still leaning back against the countertop.

"What? No."

More beckoning with his fingertips. "Are you afraid?"

"Of course not. Why would I be afraid?"

He arched his brows.

"Okay, what?" she asked, moving over to him.

He put his arms around her and pulled her flush against his body, between his spread legs. "I've been waiting to do this all morning," he murmured against her ear, then moved to her lips.

Then he kissed her.

And kissed her.

And kissed her.

Until her knees started to buckle and he lifted her up and, with a quick turn, had her sitting on the counter and him standing between her legs.

Oh, my!

He smiled.

"Are my eyes rolling back in my head?"

He laughed. "That good, huh?"

"You know it is, you rascal." She pretended to slap his shoulder.

"It is for me, too, darlin'," he said with a sudden serious expression on his face. "Can I can come back tonight?"

"Oh, Justin! We were lucky this time, but I can't have people knowing you're here all night."

"How about if I promise to leave before morning?"

She hesitated, and he kissed her again, accompanied by a grinding of his erection against her lady parts. Her eyes were definitely rolling back in her head now. He left soon after that. She hadn't told him that he could return. But she hadn't said no, either.

Louise couldn't explain her actions. It wasn't like her to take such chances. Maybe she had more Cajun Sass in her than she'd imagined.

CHAPTER 7

Can't help falling in love...

 *L*ouise had been seeing Justin for two weeks, and, despite her best intentions, she was definitely falling in love.

She loved how he looked...what woman wouldn't? She loved the way he made love, as caring about her needs as his own. She loved how smart he was and dedicated to a noble profession, even if he did raise an eyebrow on occasion at some of her more far-fetched, but effective, herbal potions. She loved how sensitive he was in dealing with Adèle; he'd spent one whole afternoon with her, teaching her how to catch crawfish with a leafy branch while Louise was busy preserving two dozen jars of fig jam to be sold at the general store.

Yes, he was arrogant and aggressive. When he wanted something, he went after it, whether it be a medical career or a woman. She couldn't exactly criticize him for that.

And, yes, it was crazy to fall for a guy who wouldn't be around for much longer. Deep down, she was hoping he might choose to come back here to practice. A far-off dream. Maybe she should call on St. Jude for a little help, but he had been oddly silent of late.

She hadn't said those three magic words to Justin, not out loud, and might not ever do so, because she had no idea if Justin reciprocated her feelings. And the clock was ticking down on the time left before he had to return north.

Oh, he cared about her. She was sure of that. Why else would he show up almost every night and leave before dawn? For the sex, of course. But he came during the day, as well, when he was able. Every spare minute he got, he spent with her, even when he had to share her with Adèle.

She noticed the way he looked at her sometimes when he thought she wasn't looking. Confused and besotted would be her description. Not that she wasn't gazing at him in the same way.

There was a kind of awareness between them whenever they were in the same room or vicinity, almost like an invisible bond, or magnetic field. Crazy, that's what it was. All they could do was smile at each other whenever it happened. It happened a lot.

And he couldn't stop touching her, even outside the bedroom. Holding her hand. Grazing her shoulder as he passed by. Trailing his fingertips over her bare arm. And quick kisses whenever anyone, including Adèle, was around; longer ones when he could get away with it.

Bottom line: There was no accounting for love. She might have locked the doors of her heart after her Big Grief, but she should have known that love had a way of sneaking in through a window left open accidentally, even when the doors were closed.

She sighed and finished up her make-up. She was going out with Justin on their first real date, as in out in public, accompanying him to his brother's wedding. Well, not the wedding ceremony itself at Our Lady of the Bayou Church. She'd opted out of that since Justin would be so busy with his best man duties. But she had agreed to go with him to the reception at the Pelican Country Club, which was as highbrow as you got here on the bayou. The bride's family was paying for the affair, and apparently they could afford it, the mother coming from old Louisiana money.

The bayou grapevine, aka gossip network, must be working overtime with news of Justin and Louise "seeing" each other, even as discreet as they'd been. Surely, customers of Louise's had seen Justin here during the day. Adèle had probably mentioned Justin's name when visiting her friends. Justin's parents and brother had to wonder where he was spending so much time on his days off work. But so far, no one had said anything to either of them.

As nervous as she was about tonight, she was also excited. There would be music and dancing, and Louise loved to dance, although she hadn't done much since the days of the USO in New Orleans. Justin promised that he could do a wicked Cajun two-step, which she didn't doubt. If he danced as well as he did other things, well, ooh la la!

She took one last look at herself in the full-length mirror on the back of her bedroom door. The new dress she'd bought fit her perfectly; it was a multi-colored greenish-blue chiffon dress with spaghetti straps, fitted on top but full and swirly from the waist to mid-calf hem. *Can anyone say dancing?* A wide, sparkly silver belt cinched in her waist and was matched with silver peep-toe high heels. Her hair was loose and hung in shiny dark curls down to her shoulders, but was pulled off her face with silver combs, making her look girlish and younger than her twenty-five years. Her only jewelry was a small silver cross on a chain around her neck.

It was a fun outfit.

The icing on the cake, which was her, came with the special care she'd taken with her make-up. Nothing outwardly sluttish. But a little bit wicked...long mascaraed eye lashes, crimson lipstick, a hint of rouge.

Raising her chin, she checked herself out in various poses. Hand on left hip, extended right foot, a Hollywood pin-up pose. A full circle pivot which raised her dress above her knees, like a dance move. Both hands behind her neck with a sultry expression on her face. With her back to the mirror, glancing back over her shoulder.

Cajun Sass, guar-an-teed, she decided.

When Justin arrived ten minutes later, he said "Wow!" on first seeing her all dolled up. He took her hand and raised it, making her do a little swirl so he get the full effect of her dress.

"You approve?" she asked, saucily.

"And then some." He kissed his fingertips and blew on them to show just how hot she was.

She smiled, returning his full body study, thinking that he was the epitome of Cajun Brass in his white tuxedo with a black bow tie and cummerbund, a pink carnation pinned to the lapel. All that white was a nice contrast to his darkly tanned skin. He'd obviously gotten a haircut that morning and a barber shave; he still smelled of aftershave.

"What are you smilin' about, *chère?*" he asked after giving her a hello kiss.

"I was jist thinkin' before you came that I was going for a Cajun Sass look t'night. And then, here you come, all Cajun Brass." She repeated his gesture of kissing her fingertips and blowing on them to demonstrate his own steam heat.

He laughed. "Cajun Sass and Cajun Brass. I like that combination." He waggled his eyebrows at her.

She locked up the house then. Adèle was staying overnight with her friend Anna Belle, with a promise that Anna Belle could stay here some night. And they were off to the reception in Houma with Justin driving his mother's cleaned and polished DeSoto, which had been decorated with crepe paper as part of the wedding party.

Once they were on their way, with Louise sitting real close to Justin, she asked, "How was the wedding so far?"

"Good, I suppose. A little hoity-toity for my taste, but then, nobody asked me."

"What do you mean by hoity-toity?"

"First of all, there were eight ushers and eight bridesmaids, in addition to the best man, maid of honor, and flower girl and boy. Then, there are these tuxedos which makes us look like a bunch of ice cream men. No priest for the ceremony would do. Had to call in a bishop friend of the family. There were enough flowers that the church smelled like a florist shop. And did I mention the limos? And then—"

"Enough!" She laughed. "I get the message. How many people are going to be at this extravaganza?"

"Two hundred."

"You're kidding! I didn't think there were that many people here on the bayou."

"Oh, they're from all over, believe me. Some big shots among them."

"I'm beginning to think I'm underdressed for this party, which is sure to be swanky. At the least, I should have put on my diamonds."

"You have diamonds?"

"Of course," she said. "Rhinestones, but they look real. Only a jeweler would know."

"You look perfect the way you are. Beautiful, as always. But different somehow."

"It's the make-up. I usually don't wear much. Or I wear enough to look like I'm not wearing any."

He looked her way and shook his head. "Nope. It's the dress. Or those killer high heels, which I have plans for later." He winked at her.

"I wonder if they're the same plans I have." She winked back at him.

He laced the fingers of his right hand with her left, and squeezed before laying their closed double fist on his thigh. "You never let me get away with anything, do you?"

She didn't know about that. It seemed to her as if he was going away soon, no matter what. That was the same as "getting away," wasn't it? She didn't say that, though. Instead, she told him, "That's the key to Cajun Sass, honey."

"What is it with you and that Cajun Sass stuff?"

She just smiled.

~

LOVE WAS IN THE AIR...

Justin was excited to show off Louise at the wedding reception because, frankly, he'd fallen hook, line, and sinker for the woman, and he wanted his family and friends to like her as much as he did.

Like? Hah! He was in love, all right, for the first time in his thirty years. Oh, he'd had all the usual teenage crushes and several long-term (like three months max) affairs, but he'd never felt like this. He couldn't imagine the rest of his life without Louise in it. The logistics of it would have to be worked out, but he was confident that love would out.

Not that he'd said any of this to Louise. Yet. He was waiting for the perfect moment. Hopefully tonight.

"Are you as nervous as I am?" she asked.

They were in the circular driveway of the country club, two cars behind the valet stand waiting their turn.

"No, why would you be nervous? These people are the same as you and me. Maybe with deeper pockets, but that doesn't make them better."

"I don't care about that," she said with a wave of her hand.

She was sitting as close to him as he could get her, with his right arm over her bare shoulders. Every time she moved, he got a whiff of her rose bath oil, which sent a message direct to his favorite body part. Would he be like that Pavlov dog from now on? Every time he smelled a rose, he'd get a hard-on?

"I'm nervous because you and I are out in public for the first time," she continued. "We've been discreet so far. I don't want everyone knowin' about the hanky panky we've been engagin' in."

He had to smile at her choice of words and squeezed her shoulder. "They probably have their suspicions anyhow. You know how bayou folks are, mindin' everyone's business." He laughed and said, "If your daddy were alive, he'd be askin' my intentions."

She elbowed him in the side

They arrived at the valet stand. He got out to get his ticket while another attendant opened the door for Louise. He took her hand and led her forward.

"Wow!" she remarked as they walked up the wide steps of the old rice plantation house complete with columns and verandahs. The mansion had been converted to a golf club with a wrap-around terrace giving access to the interior through a half-dozen sets of French doors.

"I feel like Cinderella just arriving at the ball," she said.

"Does that make me Prince Charming?" he asked with a grin.

"Oh, you a charmer, all right, *cher*," she drawled.

"You'd better not lose your shoe."

"Me, I'm more worried about turnin' into a pumpkin."

They both laughed and entered the crowd. The cocktail hour was still going on, so, people were scattered about in small groups both here on the terrace and in the reception rooms.

He recognized some of them, and Louise knew even more. They were constantly stopped for bits of conversation while he led her toward his parents and his brother and his new bride.

"Justin! Congratulations on your upcoming graduation."

"Louise! How good to see you out and about. Are you still making those herbal remedies?"

"You must meet my niece, Justin. She's a nurse."

"What a lovely dress, Louise! Where did you buy it?"

"Now that you're gonna be a doc-tor, Justin, you'll need an investment advisor for all the moolah you'll be rakin' in. Come see me, eh? Ha, ha, ha."

"Isn't it time to trade in that old jalopy of yours, Louise? Ha, ha, ha!" said Dan Doucet from Dapper Dan's Used Cars With Oomph. "Drop in to my lot on Monday and I'll give you a deal, guar-an-teed! I have one with a rumble seat you might like."

The place was decorated to the nines in ribbons and flowers, the round tables set with silver and china and crystal goblets. White-gloved waiters were walking around with trays of wines in stemmed glasses and bite-size appetizers. Swanky, just like Louise had predicted. His parents never would have been able to afford something like this.

After seeing this spread, he was finding it hard to

believe that Lily Rose would be satisfied operating a little beauty salon inside the general store. He suspected his brother would have his hands full down the road, but that was their problem, not his.

Once he got to the area in front of the head table where his parents' group was standing, he introduced Louise to the Fortiers, George and Sonia, as a well-known bayou folk healer. He could tell it surprised Louise that he showed pride in her work.

Louise would probably have something to say later about how George had a good twenty years on his wife. His brother Leon winked at him as he greeted Louise, his dad gave her a warm handshake, acknowledging to everyone around that he not only knew Louise well but that he worked with her, and his mother gave her a long hug, probably hoping that Louise would be the key to Justin's coming back to the bayou.

The Fortiers, including Lily Rose, were a little snooty in their greetings, excusing themselves to go off to meet someone important who'd just arrived, taking Leon with them. Not that they'd said it in quite that way. More like subtle snobbery. The whole bunch of them and their like thought the sun came up every day just to hear them crow.

His dad muttered something about people who were too big for their britches.

His mother said, "Shh!"

His dad persisted, "Didja see the size of them tiny sandwiches they're passin' around? 'Bout the size of mah thumb. Wouldn't fill the stomach of a June bug. And some of 'em are filled with grass."

"Thass water cress," his mother explained.

"Lak I said, grass. I coulda sent over twenty pounds of boudin sausage, or some lunch meat, if I'd known they'd be so skimpy."

"I caint believe you asked for a beer."

"I caint believe they brought it to me in some fancy-pancy crystal glass."

Justin and Louise looked at each other and smiled.

"Listen, honey," he said to Louise a short time later. "I have to sit at the head table during dinner, but I'll join you when the dancing starts."

"I'm holding you to that."

He'd promised her a night of dancing, and he intended to follow through, once his commitments were over. In the meantime, he led her to one of the tables up front where there was a name tag in front of her plate. She would be sitting with his parents, his Uncle Joe and Aunt Lizzie from Lafayette, his grandmother Marion Boudreaux, Dr. Clovis LeDeux, and Alan Despain, a new young lawyer from Houma, who was looking at Louise with more interest than Justin liked.

After seating Louise, he leaned down and gave her a kiss, in front of one and all, dammit, and whispered, "See you soon. Save the first dance for me."

He could tell by her blush that his public kiss embarrassed her. But only a little, he suspected; she was in what she called her Cajun Sass mood.

Before he left, Dr. Clovis, who was sitting on Louise's right, said, "Did your young man tell you I offered him a job?"

"Noooo." Louise looked up at Justin in question.

"A full partnership with me in my practice, and mebbe even a home in the long run. Hasn't given me an answer, though." The doctor winked at her, as if she could convince Justin, and took a sip of what was probably his third or fourth bourbon on the rocks.

Not only was Louise interested in what Dr. Clovis had said, but his parents were listening avidly, too. Damn the man for spilling the beans. Justin hadn't made a decision, and the old guy knew it good and well.

"You only made the offer a few days ago, Dr. Clovis," Justin pointed out.

Fortunately, an announcement over the microphone said, "Everyone to their seats, please. Dinner will be served shortly." But Justin knew he'd have some explaining to do later. A band had arrived and was setting up on a dais across the large room.

Justin squeezed Louise's shoulder and left for his seat at the head table.

It took more than an hour before Justin was able to be with Louise again, following a meal that he had to admit was excellent—filet mignon and fresh Gulf shrimp—a bunch of speeches, champagne toasts, and cutting of the cake, which someone whispered had cost five hundred dollars. The Fortiers had opted out of some of the traditional Cajun wedding rituals, probably too lowdown for the Fortier's highbrow life style.

By the time he got free of his duties, the dancing was well underway, and Louise was already out on the dance floor, enjoying herself. Not just with the stupid lawyer, but every eligible bachelor at this dig had her in his crosshairs. Like he'd thought, that dress of hers exposed a good amount of her legs, including some of her lower thighs, when her partners twirled her around. Which they did. A lot. Probably deliberately. Dammit!

The musicians alternated between big band music and Cajun songs. Just then, they segued from "In the Mood," to "Jolie Blon." Justin took that as his cue to cut in on Louise and her partner.

"Hey, Hank," he said. Hank Ishler, a teacher at the community college, was one of the ushers, a friend of Leon's. "Thanks for taking care of my girl while I was busy." Justin nudged him aside with his hip and took Louise in his arms. Hank gaped at him, as if to say, "What just happened?"

Justin didn't care. He spun Louise around once, then tugged her closer into his arms, settling into a slow two-step. He had his arms looped around her waist; she had her hands laced behind his neck. He smiled at the sheer pleasure he felt just holding Louise. "Sorry it took so long."

"That's okay. I've been dancing."

"I noticed," he said, pretending to be annoyed.

She laughed. "I didn't realize I would know so many people here."

"It's a small world, as the saying goes."

"And the bayou is an even smaller world."

"Yep!"

"Speaking of which…" She tilted her head in question, studying his face. "You never mentioned that Dr. Clovis offered you a partnership here on the bayou."

Uh-oh! He'd deliberately not told Louise or anyone else, not even his parents, about Dr. Clovis's offer because he knew they'd get their hopes up, and he was ninety-nine percent sure that he wouldn't accept. After all his years of hard work, he would feel as if he was settling for less than his capabilities if he accepted a general practice in a back-woods office with an elderly alcoholic for a partner, without a major hospital nearby. On the other hand, there was talk of a new Terrebonne General Medical Center being built in Houma in the next few years. He would be in on the ground floor if he was already settled here.

"Nothing's been decided," he told her. "I still have to get through my medical exams."

"Still, it's a compliment to you, isn't it?"

"It is," he admitted. "But enough serious stuff for tonight." He pulled her even closer into his arms. With high heels on…the first she'd worn around him…he still had a good four inches on her, but they were on a more level playing field, so to speak. And his batter was up and ready to hit a home run, so to speak. He grinned against her hair, deciding he wouldn't share that crude thought with her.

Instead, he pulled back slightly to look at her. "I know you were reluctant to come to this affair tonight, *chère*. But looks to me like you're havin' a good time."

"*Mais oui!* But I expect it to get better now."

And it did.

He made sure of that.

And so did she.

Holy crawfish, so did she!

God bless Cajun Sass.

CHAPTER 8

With hope, anything is possible. Right, St. Jude?...

"I think I love you," Justin said, leaning over her the next morning. His hair was bed-mussed, or was that sex-mussed? There was a bite mark on his one shoulder. And his mouth appeared a bit bruised from a whole lot of kissing. In other words, he looked wonderful. And why wouldn't he? They'd made love on practically every surface in her cottage since they'd arrived home just before midnight, including her bed, finally, where they were now.

He'd already gone through one of those tins of prophy-lactics and was halfway through a second. At this rate, she'd laughingly told him last night, "You should buy stock in the company that makes them."

He'd responded, "Right now, I'm so poor I can barely pay attention, let alone pay for stocks. Ha, ha, ha! But, yeah, once I'm earning some real money, and my checks no longer bounce, I'll sure thing invest in rubbers. Bounce, rubbers, get it? Ha, ha, ha!"

Justin had a great sense of humor, or so he thought. Louise just shook her head at this particularly sorry attempt of his at levity.

She stretched and thought about getting up, but there really was no need for rush on either of their parts, it being a Sunday. Her car sat in the driveway, and his mother's car was parked in the detached garage (just barely, considering its size). So, they were safe from nosy neighbors or passersby, for now. His parents presumably thought he went back to his apartment in New Orleans after dropping her off.

"Did you hear what I said, Louise? I think I love you. So much it kind of scares me."

Oh, she'd heard him, all right. Loud and clear. "Think?" she asked with an exaggerated frown.

His face flushed with color as he realized his mistake. "I know I love you, but I think I'm *in love* with you, too."

"Am I supposed to be pleased at that backward explanation?"

"You know what I mean." He waited for her to say something then, and when she didn't, he nipped her chin with his teeth and prodded, "Well?"

Truth to tell, she knew she was in love, but she wasn't about to be the first one to say it. She was basking in the glow, though. Ever since she'd learned that Justin was offered an opportunity to practice medicine right here on the bayou, the doors of her heart had flown open. Any reservations she'd had about him were gone. It was a dream come true, a life she could only hope for before. Now, despite her best intentions, she found herself fantasizing about the life they could have together. Him a doctor, her a folk healer, a combination that would succeed because of its very uniqueness. In fact, they complemented each other professionally. She had a vision of herself with Justin, Adèle, and maybe one or two other children. Maybe they would even be living in Dr. Clovis's mansion once he retired, as the old guy had hinted. Or they could put an addition onto her cottage.

Hope was a wonderful thing.

But for now, she knew Justin was waiting for her response to his declaration. "I *think* I'm in love with you, too," she said, leaning up to give him a quick kiss.

"Ouch! I see how that sounds." He rolled her over so that she lay on top of him, bare skin to bare skin. "I have an idea for what we can do today."

She laughed. "You and your ideas."

He pinched her buttock and said, "Not that kind of idea, although now that you mention it…"

A half hour later, he was on his back, and she was on her side, tucked under his arm, both of them sated. Turned out it was a really good idea.

"What I was going to suggest, Miss Know-It-All, before you so rudely diverted my attention is—"

"Me? You're the one who's insatiable."

"Thank you," he said, as if that was a compliment. "Anyway, let's spend the day at the beach. We can pick up Adèle and go to Grand Isle. What do you say?"

"That sounds wonderful." She was especially touched that he picked an activity that would include Adèle. "But don't you have to study?"

"I can bring my books with me."

By noon, they crossed the causeway which connected the mainland to the narrow barrier island, which was a mere eight miles long and at most a mile and a half wide in spots. Another hour later, and the three of them were settled on the beach at Grand Isle. Louise was sitting on a heavy woven blanket watching Justin as he held Adèle's hand, running along the edge of the water, laughing as she shrieked every time she got wet from all the splashing, inching farther and farther out until finally Justin quickly dunked them both. Instead of being frightened, Adèle came up with a big smile on her little face. She was a beginning swimmer, at the dog paddling stage, but a little water didn't bother her.

Louise smiled and leaned back on her elbows. She was filled with such a feeling of utter peace. Hope did that to a person, she supposed.

Suddenly, for the first time in weeks, that voice spoke in her head. St. Jude. *Well, thou art partly right. Actually, it is faith, hope, and love, according to the Bible.*

Picky, picky!

Be careful what you wish for, child.

Child? I'm hardly a child.

We've noticed.

Was he referring to the sex? *Uh-oh.*

Thou can sayeth that again!

The inner voice quieted when Justin called out to her, Adèle sitting on his shoulders as they approached, both of them waving wildly. "Tante Lulu! Tante Lulu! Look at me. Ahm a giant." Adèle called out.

"And I'm a giant's stepstool," Justin said with a grin.

The good thing about being on a beach, she decided then, was that you could ogle a man's body, head to toe and everywhere in between, without appearing to be a pervert. And Justin's body was a work of art in his low-riding swimming trunks, and nothing more, to be admired...and, yes, ogled. He wasn't overly muscular, like some athletes or body builders, but he did have muscles in all the right places, including his wide shoulders, his rippled abdomen, and, well, lots of places.

Even his big, narrow feet were kind of sexy.

And his belly button? Well, it gave her ideas that would

make a strip tease artist like Gypsy Rose Lee blush.

Truly, this man...her lover...was hotter than a jalapeno's coochie.

Justin grinned at her, noticing her perusal, and gave back an equal full-body survey to her body in her red and white striped, one-piece, halter bathing suit in that new, stretchy material that clung to a lady's curves like a girdle, or made it appear there were curves when there were not. Suddenly, the modest suit felt transparent. The blush which still heated her cheeks probably matched her cherry-red toenails which matched her lipstick and the red stripe in her suit.

When Justin got to the blanket, he set Adèle on the sand, and the two of them shook their bodies like wet dogs, spraying her with cold droplets.

She laughed. The cold spray was welcome in this ninety-degree heat.

"Is anybody hungry?" she asked as the two of them toweled themselves dry before dropping down to the blanket.

"Ahm so hon-gry Ah could eat an alligator," Justin said, giving a gator-like roar.

Adèle giggled and looked up adoringly at Justin, her new best pal. "Ahm so hon-gry Ah could eat a skunk," she added.

"Eew!" Louise remarked as she opened the metal ice chest she'd brought with them and began to lay out a picnic feast of fried chicken, buttered biscuits, potato salad, wedges of watermelon, and sweet tea.

An hour later, all the remaining food had been put away, and Adèle was sitting in the sand, hard at work with bucket and shovel, while Justin leaned back on the pillow he'd made of several rolled towels, an open Advanced Physiology book propped on his chest.

"I think I'll go for a walk," she said. "Anyone want to join me?"

Neither Justin nor Adèle were budging. So, Louise took off on her own, which was fine. She preferred this alone time to think, even pray, and what a place to meditate! Just as Louise loved her bayou home and its surroundings, she also had a fondness for Grand Isle, where she and her family had spent many summer days as they were growing up. While Louise and her much older brother Frank played in the waves, and their mother sunned herself on the white sandy beach, her father, a shrimp fisherman, went off on a busman's holiday, fishing off the famous four-hundred-foot pier that led out onto the Gulf of Mexico, for the more than two hundred species of fish that reportedly abounded there. They always returned home with their metal ice chest filled with fish, fileted on the spot, to be enjoyed over the next few days. Red and black drum, flounder, *sac-au-lait*, lots of specks, or speckled trout, and a dozen other types, depending on the season or the time of day caught. Once her father had caught a twenty-pound Big Bull Red, so large it wouldn't fit in the ice chest. They'd eaten fish "five ways to Sunday," in her mother's words, over the summer months, even after sharing half with a neighbor who'd been laid off from his factory job.

In a way, Grand Isle was symbolic of the Cajun inhabitants of southern Louisiana. Survivors. The barrier island had been hit repeatedly by destructive hurricanes over the centuries, including the one made most famous by Kate Chopin's scandalous book, "The Awakening," and it always came back. Just like the Cajuns, or Acadians, who had been kicked out of several countries and forced to live in the supposedly uninhabitable swamps of Louisiana, where they not only survived but developed their own foods, music, and culture which quickly matched their Creole competitors. In fact, just like Louise herself, who'd suffered through her Big Grief over the loss of Phillipe, the birth of an illegitimate child, the death of her father, brother, and mother, poverty, and the struggles with running her own business.

But now what? That's what Louise wanted to ponder as she strolled the beach. Until Justin brought up his plans for the future, Louise would feel uncomfortable making plans of her own. But it was hard not to be hopeful. He'd told her last night that they would discuss Dr. Clovis's offer later. But so far, nothing.

What was Justin waiting for anyhow?

While she walked and enjoyed the scenery, she was apparently the scenery for some people on the beach… men, in particular. She had to wonder if it was her recently adopted Cajun Sass that was apparent, in attitude more than anything else. It couldn't be her bathing suit. It was no more revealing than any other one on the beach. And it couldn't be her body, either, which was fine, but nothing overtly sexual, in her opinion. But maybe a combination of all three. Who could figure out the male mind?

A thought occurred to her suddenly. *Can men sniff out a woman who is sexually active? Do they have a built-in radar for easy girls? Lordy, Lordy, do I give off a certain slut scent?*

The first one who approached her looked about sixteen, freckles and all. "Hey, darlin', don't I know you from somewhere?" His voice cracked in the middle of his sentence.

She smiled and continued walking. He fast-walked to keep up with her, which wasn't difficult with her being so much shorter.

"Seriously?" she said. "Don't you need to go do your homework or something?"

"I don't have homework in the summer," he replied before he realized what he'd admitted.

Louise didn't want to embarrass the kid but she also didn't want him tagging along. "Listen, sweetie, you're cute and all that, but my husband's a dock worker, and he gets real jealous. Broke the jaw of the last guy who winked at me."

"Wi-wink?" he stuttered.

Then, there was the guy leaning against a sign announcing the hours that the beach was open to the public. A lot older than her first Lothario. Maybe thirty-five, or even forty. Arms folded over an impressive chest, ankles crossed, he wore dark sunglasses, which he slid halfway down his nose to give her a better scrutiny. He was the epitome of Cajun rascal; she could tell that even before he opened his mouth and drawled, "*Chère*, you look good enough to eat. Lak a Christmas candy cane. Lak sweet beignets at Café du Monde."

She laughed. "Does that line work for you, *cher*?"

He laughed back at her and shrugged, "Sometimes, yes. Sometimes, no."

"Well, this time it's a 'no'. Good luck, *mon ami*."

He gave her a smart salute and no doubt watched her behind as she turned and walked back the way she'd come. She gave her hips a little extra wiggle just because she was feeling sassy.

She heard her next "pursuer" before he spoke.

"Hey, baby," pant, pant, "where you been," pant, pant, "all my life?" pant, pant, pant, pant.

She stopped walking, fearing the short, fat, sixty-if-he-was-a-day gentleman tracking her would have a heart attack on the beach. That's when she got a look-see at the old guy's attire. One of those stretchy men's bathing suits that barely covered their you-know-what or the crack in the back. His belly hung halfway over what pretty much looked like a sling for a banana. And he had enough gray hair on his chest and arms to knit a sweater.

Is this what I'm coming to? she wondered.

Then she answered her sassy Cajun self, *Heck, no!*

"Sit down, Pops, and rest on your 'laurels'," she advised and continued on her way, chuckling.

When she got back to her blanket, she found Justin fast asleep on his back, the book still open on his chest, probably at the same page. And Adèle was asleep as well, her face on Justin's shoulder, her little pink ruffled bottom in the air, his hand resting on her mop of still-damp curly hair. They could have been father and daughter. In fact, for a brief second, it almost looked like Phillipe lying there.

Is it possible that Phillipe sent Justin to me? That he wants me to find another love? That he chose a father for his child?

Whaaat? Forget Cajun Sass. I'm going Cajun Crazy.

Bless my heart!

～

AND THEN THE **other shoe dropped...**

Justin was not being fair with his silence. Not to Louise, not to his parents, and not to Doctor Clovis, all of whom had an interest in his future plans. But, dammit, he was waiting to hear about something important. It was a longshot that would probably never pay off, but, man, it could be so life-altering that he had to give it a chance.

In the meantime, he was studying almost full-time for his medical boards which he would take in ten more days. He'd already tied up the loose ends of his residency at the hospital and only had a few more shifts to handle before he was done.

It was almost two weeks since the wedding and his day

at Grand Isle, but he'd only been able to get back to Houma a few times for in-and-out visits…literally, in Louise's case. With his parents, it was usually a quick dinner before he was off. His brother and his bride would return soon from their extended honeymoon to Europe, which was already recovering from the war. It had been a wedding gift from the Fortiers.

In mid-afternoon, there was a knock on the door of the Creole cottage he shared with his roommate, Barry Chauvin, a fellow resident at the hospital from LSU. He heard the knock from his small bedroom upstairs, but didn't bother to go down since he knew Barry was at home, studying for his own exams. Within minutes, Barry called out from the stairway, "Yo, Boudreaux! You got company."

To his shock, it was his mother. All dressed up in her Sunday clothes—on a weekday—a pretty floral, belted dress with low-heeled white pumps. Minus the usual white butcher's apron that she wore in the store. Her gray-streaked brown hair was done up in the neat Victory Roll hairstyle made popular during the war; she must have come here directly from the beauty parlor.

After giving her a warm hug, he said, "Mama, what you doin' here? Doan tell me you were just passin' by. I have your car here. Is Daddy with you?"

"No, no. Jist me. Drove Leon's car. Did a little shoppin' at Holmes Department Store, then decided to come visit you. Cain't a mother visit her oldest son without askin'?"

There had to be more than that.

"Are you sick? Is Daddy sick?"

She shook her head as he settled her onto the upholstered davenport in the small living room while he sat beside her.

"Would you like something to drink? Sweet tea? Lemonade? There's probably coffee, too. I've been drinking so much coffee while I study that I'm 'bout to turn into a coffee bean."

"You work so hard." She patted him on the knee. "No, nothin' to drink." She stared around the room then and remarked, "You know the history of these Creole cottages, dontcha?" He nodded, but still she went on to explain, "Back before the Big War," (*to Southerners, the Big War referred not to World War I or II but to the Civil War*), "the white plantation owners would go to the Quadroon Balls where they would pick out mixed race young women to be their *placées*, or common-law wives. All legal and accepted. They bought them houses, jist like this one, and signed contracts to raise their children and provide for them for life, or until they got tired of them. Tsk, tsk, tsk! A horrible practice, *plaçage* was! Use 'em and lose 'em, as you young folks say today. Those poor women!"

Justin frowned. He had no idea what this visit was really about.

"I'm worried about Louise...and that niece of hers."

Whaaat? That was the last thing he'd expected. "Why?"

His mother raised her eyebrows at him. "Men! Yer brains are different from women's, thass fer sure."

That was true, to some extent, but not in the way his mother probably meant. Justin decided not to give her an anatomy lesson. "What does that have to do with Louise or Adèle?"

Instead of answering his question, his mother veered off in another direction. "Such a sweet chile, that Adèle. I allus wondered why she didn't live with her mother, Patti Rivard, or why her mother never came to visit, even if she did give her baby up. Some women jist ain't motherly, I guess." His mother shrugged.

"I didn't know Adèle's mother was around."

"Oh, she's not. Lives in Mexico, I think. Has ever since

she jilted her husband Frank while he was in a prison camp during the war and ran off with some soldier who went AWOL. That was before Frank died. Such a scandal it was at the time."

"Mama! Where do you hear all these things?"

"The ladies of the Altar and Rosary Society. We meet fer lunch every first Friday of the month after low mass."

Ah! The bayou grapevine. Gossip central.

"Patti's second cousin, Simone Sonnier, who lives in Biloxi, has a great-aunt who lives in Houma."

"And that great-aunt belongs to the Altar and Rosary Society," Justin guessed.

"Oh, no! That great-aunt's third cousin is the one I know. Beulah Ann Sonnier. Remember her? She has a hairy wart on her chin the size of a cherry. You kids allus thought she was a witch."

Justin rolled his eyes at the convoluted relationships on the bayou which were perfectly understandable to Cajuns, but no one else.

"Mebbe you could meet up with Beulah Ann, kind of accidental, and mention that you, bein' a doctor and all, could cut that big ol' wart off, lickety-split."

He looked at his mother with horror. "First of all, how in the world do you imagine that I could just run into Beulah Ann Sonnier?"

"At church?"

He ignored that suggestion and went on, "Secondly, I am not quite a doctor yet. And third, you don't just cut off a wart that size. We're talking anesthetic and stitches, and—"

His mother waved a hand dismissively. "You'll be a doctor in a couple weeks. Have I mentioned how proud I am of you?" She beamed at him.

"Mama! Can you stop changing the subject? You started

by saying you're worried about Louise."

She nodded and gave him a look of disapproval.

So much for her motherly pride.

"I'm afraid you're going to hurt Louise."

"How?'

"Justin, it's obvious to me, if it's not to everyone else, that you do not want to come back to the bayou."

"I wouldn't say that, exactly."

"Is it Dr. Clovis that's put you off? I know he's a lot to handle."

He shook his head. "I like Dr. Clovis, despite all his warts."

She didn't even smile at his joke.

"It's family medicine that I'm not sure about," he explained.

She tilted her head to the side.

"I'm thinking about specializing."

"In what?"

He shrugged, as if uncertain, although he was more than certain.

"Oh, good Lord! That would mean more schooling, wouldn't it?"

He nodded. "Possibly three more years." At the expression of worry on her face, he patted her arm. "Don't worry. I wouldn't do it unless I got a scholarship. I wouldn't ask you and Dad for more help."

"It's not that. We're happy to help when we can."

"And you've done plenty. Anyhow, Mama, nothing is decided."

"Does Louise know about all this?"

"Hmm. Not exactly."

His mother blew out an exhale of disgust. "See, Louise is going to be hurt. Do you love her?"

"Yes," he said without hesitation.

"And does she love you?"

I think so. "Yes."

"Does she think you're going to settle here in Loo-zee-anna?"

"She probably hopes…as you have."

"Well, consider how disappointed I am and multiply that by a hundred for Louise."

"Stop worrying, Mama. Nothing is settled yet," he told her when she finally left after gaining a promise from him to return on Sunday for a Welcome Home dinner for his brother Leon and Lily Rose. He wasn't looking forward to the event, which would probably involve a slide show of all the sites they'd visited in Europe, but he'd do it to please his mother.

Later that day, there was another knock on the door.

Who could it be now?

Since his roommate was out now, he took the stairs two at a time, and opened the door to find a mailman standing on the porch, holding a special delivery. Justin signed for the oversized envelope.

"Hope it's good news," the man said.

"Me, too," Justin replied.

Once back inside, he stared at the envelope for a long moment. It was addressed to Dr. Justin Boudreaux. A bit premature, that, but who was he to complain? The return address was a hospital in Chicago, as he'd expected.

At first, he was afraid to open the envelope. As long as it remained closed, he still had hope. But wait, why was he being so negative? He tore the envelope open and quickly scanned the contents.

Slowly, a smile emerged on his face, and he let out a whoop of happiness. His future was sealed! Solid gold!

Now, to convince Louise that she should share in his future.

CHAPTER 9

Stormy weather...

$\mathcal{L}$ ouise was making Adèle's favorite Cajun spaghetti and meatballs, a mix of andouille sausage with ground beef, and a dash of tabasco in the sauce, when she heard a car crunch over the clamshells in the driveway. Looking out the window, she saw Justin emerge from his mother's DeSoto. She hadn't expected him today. And what was it with the huge bouquet of flowers he was carrying in one hand and a bottle of what looked like champagne in the other?

What does it mean?

Oh. He must have accepted Dr. Clovis's offer and he's come to celebrate with me.

She smiled and did a little dance in place.

"Tante Lulu! It's Jus-tin," Adèle yelled from the porch where she'd been playing with her Mr. Potato Head.

By the time Louise turned down the heat on her sauce and got to the door, Justin was standing there with a big grin on his face and Adèle's little arms wrapped around his thighs. Despite the two or more days of whiskers on his face, and his wrinkled shorts and T-shirt, he looked hotter than a movie star. Like that James Dean, but better. Rebel with a cause.

He handed her the bouquet and the bottle and leaned down to give her a kiss...a kiss that lasted a little longer than it should have, considering the bundle still hanging on his leg.

"Adèle, sweetheart, let Justin go. Give him a chance to catch his breath."

"Okay," Adèle said, scuffling her shoe on the porch floor.

"Hey, Short Stuff, here's a little present for you, too." He handed her a book that apparently had sound effects. As Adèle flicked through the pages, Louise heard a cow moo, and a cat meow. "Let me talk to your aunt for a few minutes, and then we can read the book together. Or else I can help you with Mr. Potato Head. I make a swell Sweet Potato Head."

Adèle's eyes lit up and she said, "Yippee!" She held onto the book even as she went back to her Mr. Potato Head, who was looking more like Mr. Mashed Potato. Justin followed Louise inside. While she put the flowers in an oversized Mason jar in the sink, Justin opened the champagne and poured some in two St. Jude tumblers.

Louise sat next to him at the kitchen table and raised her glass to click with his. After they'd both taken a sip of their bubbly drinks, she said, "So, Mister Mysterious, what're we celebrating?"

He took one of her hands in his and kissed the knuckles. "I have the most amazing news."

She waited for him to tell her that he'd accepted Dr. Clovis's offer.

"I've been offered a residency in heart surgery at

Chicago General, one of the best teaching hospitals in the United States…maybe in the whole world."

She blinked several times, not sure she had heard right. It was totally not what she'd expected. "Chicago?" she asked. For some reason, a picture flashed into her head, one that had appeared in the *Times-Picayune* last winter showing something like three feet of snow in the "Windy City." A blizzard, it had been, which apparently wasn't unusual for that part of the country. To a bayou girl who'd at best seen snow flurries, that scenario boggled the mind.

"Are you serious? Chicago? Heart surgery? I don't understand."

He squeezed her hand and said, "Honey, this is a dream come true."

Your dream. She pulled her hand away and fiddled with the St. Jude placemat sitting on the table before her.

"I know I haven't talked about it, but it's a specialty I've been thinking about for a long time. The human heart is such a remarkable organ."

Tell me about it. Mine is beginning to develop a few cracks as you speak.

"This is a field that's expected to explode in the next few years. They're already talking about open-heart surgery where they hook a damaged heart up to a bypass machine while they operate. Hell, some people think there will be heart transplants someday. Imagine! And I would be in on the ground floor of all this medical magic." He beamed at her, expecting her to understand, to approve of his decision.

"I can see how excited you are, but, Justin, why haven't you mentioned it to me before?" *Why have you led me on to believe you might be a doctor here on the bayou one day?*

"I don't have the money to pay for that kind of specialty myself, and the opportunities for scholarships in this field are slim and highly competitive. But miracle of miracles, I've been offered a full-ride scholarship, including living expenses."

Um, that isn't exactly what We consider miracles up here, St. Jude said in her head. *And believe me, I know miracles. Raising the dead, curing the lame, parting the Red Sea. Now, those were miracles!*

Honestly, the saint appeared at the most inopportune times, bless his heart. She hadn't heard from him in days, and now when all her hopes were going down the drain... Hopeless.

Bite thy tongue, girl, said the patron saint of hopeless cases.

Did I wait too long? Is it too late for a miracle?

"What did you say about miracles?" Justin asked.

"Nothing," she said, adding a *Shhh!* to her inner voice. Looking directly at Justin, she said, "That still doesn't explain why you never mentioned your interest in a heart specialty to me. We're not talking about the world. I'm the person you supposedly love. There should be no secrets, not even little ones, and this is a biggie." At the back of her mind, she felt a tiny twinge of guilt. Hadn't she been keeping a big secret from him?

"I didn't want to jinx my chances. And, besides, like I said, my chances were so remote."

He isn't taking Dr. Clovis's offer. For some reason, that thought kept hammering in her head. Apparently, the reality of it hadn't fully registered yet. "But Chicago? How long will you be there?

"At least three years."

She groaned. She couldn't help herself.

"But, honey, it's not how long *I'll* be there. How long *we'll* be there."

"What?"

"Marry me, Louise. Marry me and come to Chicago with me. Please."

She was in shock. Yes, this was what she'd wanted, what she'd been fantasizing about for weeks...to have Justin propose, but never had she expected it to come like this. In her fantasies, the proposal led to the two of them working together here on the bayou.

Sensing she was dismayed by his less-than-charming approach, Justin dropped to one knee and took both of her hands in his. "Louise Rivard, would you do me the honor of marrying me?"

Tears filled her eyes. "I don't know."

Justin flinched, taken aback. Was he really so clueless that he expected her to jump at the chances of marrying him *no matter what?* Realizing that he needed to do some damage control, he quickly said, "I love you, Louise, and I know you love me, too."

"I do, but..."

"Love conquers all, isn't that what they say?"

Is he trying to be funny? Now? Yep, clueless! "Maybe *they* weren't hit by a stumbling block the size of a bayou barge."

He rose to his feet and sat down again, facing her, but still holding onto both hands.

Compromise...that's what all the magazines said couples needed to make a relationship work. Louise searched her mind, trying to find a way that this might work, even though she wasn't sure she could live up north for that long, or wait for him here for that long. "Would you return to the bayou...well, at least Louisiana...to practice medicine after those three years?"

"I don't know. Maybe. It would depend on whether there were openings for heart surgeons."

So much for compromise. She shook her head and pulled her hands from his grasp, grabbing a St. Jude napkin to dab at her eyes. "That's not good enough, Justin. I'm sorry, but the bayou is in my blood. The Cajun community is like my family. It's who I am. I'm not a Yankee folk healer. I'm a bayou folk healer. I deal with plants that grow in the swamps, not in some city park."

"You could ship your plants there."

"My customers are here. Can you imagine a market up north for gator salve or whooping cough tea?"

"You're overthinking this. If you love me, if we love each other, we can find something for you to do. Is the bayou more important than love? Just give it a chance… give us a chance."

She ignored his pleadings. "Honestly, a vacation or short time elsewhere, maybe, but I can't see myself leaving for good. And definitely not to a big city with all that concrete." She shivered at the thought. "My soul would wither without greenery and water surrounding me."

"What if I promised we would come back after my residency is completed?"

"How could you promise that? You just said there might not be any openings."

"If I had to, I could open my own office."

"Could you afford to do that?"

"Probably not. We could sell your cottage if worst came to worst, I suppose, and rent some living space until my practice was established."

"Sell my cottage? My family home?"

"I don't know. I just know that I don't want to live without you."

"I don't want to live without you, either," she said on a sigh. "There would be so many details to be worked out."

Seeing that she was succumbing to his persuasions, he kissed her quickly and pulled her onto his lap. "There is one other problem."

She braced herself. What could be worse than leaving the bayou for years, maybe forever? Or selling her home?

"The housing provided for a married resident is what they're calling a one-bedroom apartment but is so small it's really just an efficiency...in other words, one room serving as bedroom, living room, and kitchen. Plus, the building for resident living is in a poor neighborhood."

Louise tilted her head, wondering where Justin was going with this new bit of information. It's not like she was fussy about living arrangements. Even the shabbiest of dwellings could be improved with a little paint or bright pillows. As for small, hadn't she been living in a small cottage her entire life, even when her parents and brother shared the space? "And?"

"There would be no room for Adèle. Not at first."

Louise felt as if she'd been sucker punched. She pushed out of Justin's embrace and stood, turning away from him. For a second, she couldn't breathe, just panted for breath. When she turned, her body froze, like there was ice in her veins. Justin stood, too, and looked as sad as she no doubt did.

"I thought you liked Adèle."

"I do, honey. In fact, I love her. Let me explain." He reached for her, but she stepped away.

"You love her, and yet you suggest us sashaying off to Chicago? Without her? For three years! Or do you mean forever?" Louise reeled with disbelief. His announcement that he was going to Chicago had been like a stab to the heart, but this...this exclusion of Adèle in such a dismissive way...well, that was the mortal blow.

"No, no, no! Not for three years. Just temporarily. There is a way. Just keep an open mind."

She bristled. Now he was laying this disaster on her?

"I was talking to my mother, and she mentioned that

Adèle's mother lives in Mexico, but that she has a grand-mother living in Biloxi. Why couldn't we ask her grand-mother if Adèle could stay with her until we get ourselves settled...until we can find bigger accommodations in a better neighborhood?"

The ice in her veins shot to her brain, and she felt light-headed and dizzy. "You've been talking to your mother about me?" That felt like such a betrayal of trust that Louise staggered and put a hand on the countertop to steady herself.

"It wasn't like that. My mother came to Nawleans because she was worried about you, and that's when the subject came up."

This situation just got worse and worse. "Why was she worried about me?"

Color infused his cheeks as he confessed, "She was afraid that I was going to hurt you."

"Bingo!" Louise said.

"Not like this. She thought I was going to be one of those love 'em and leave 'em kind of guys, which is clearly wrong since I'm asking you to marry me and come with me." He tried to take her in his arms once again, pleading, "Louise, I love you. You love me. We can work this out. We'll find a way."

She shook her head and stepped back a few steps. "I think you should leave, Justin."

"No, honey, we need to settle this."

She shook her head again, and the tears that had been welling in her eyes overflowed. She put a halting hand out to prevent him from getting closer.

There were tears in his eyes, too. "I've handled this badly, but please give me a chance to explain this better."

"All the explaining in the world isn't going to make any

difference. It's like my mama always said. You can't undo a burnt pudding."

"Maybe we both need to step back and think about this. I'll come back later. Tonight. I promise we'll find a way to make this work."

What he really meant was that she would find a way to compromise, Louise suspected. Which wasn't going to happen.

"No, Justin, don't come back. It breaks my heart to say this…" her voice cracked with emotion, "…but it's over. I love you, but I can't see you anymore."

"What? Why?" He was totally shocked now, and ignored her attempts to prevent him from taking her into his arms. Holding her tightly against his body, he leaned down to whisper against her ear. "No, Louise, don't say that. This isn't the end. It can't be."

For a moment, she pressed her face against his chest and relished the feel of his arms. His hands caressed her back in soothing strokes. Then he took her face in his hands and kissed her, hungrily, coaxing, unending, as if desperate to continue the kiss, lest she mention a break-up again.

Which she intended to do.

"Justin, I need you to step away so I can tell you something."

He gave her another short kiss, then released her. She went to the other side of the kitchen table, just to make sure he kept his distance.

"There's a reason why this will never be…not our marriage, not a move to Chicago for me, temporary or otherwise."

"There is no reason I'll accept, nothing could be that important."

"Adèle is my daughter," she said, "Not my niece."

~

*You always hurt **the one you love...***

Justin was finally able to talk with Louise on the phone later that night. She'd ignored his previous twelve calls, and he was ninety-nine percent sure that she would not welcome an in-person visit from him, at least for the time being. And forget about studying; his concentration wasn't worth shit at the moment.

His mother had been worried about how he might hurt Louise. What she hadn't taken into account was how hurt he would be.

"Louise, please let me talk to you. At the least, let me clarify some things. One, I love you. Period. No question. Two, it doesn't matter to me if Adèle is your child, or your niece, though I wish you had trusted me enough to tell me before. Third, I love Adèle. I would never do anything to hurt her, and, yes, I realize now how selfish it was for me to even suggest that she be separated from you, even for a short time. Fourth, I will do anything to keep you. Give up the heart surgery specialty. Accept Dr. Clovis's offer to partner with him in general medicine. Anything."

There was a silence before she asked, "Are you reading from a script?"

"Yes, dammit! My brain is so screwed up I can't think straight. I had to put my thoughts on paper or else I would have been babbling like an idiot or begging like a baby." Both of which he was doing. Dammit!

"Oh, Justin! You have to study for your medical boards. You only have a few days left."

He took her concern as a good sign. "You do care about me."

"Of course I care about you. Women aren't like men. We can't turn love on and off like a faucet."

He decided not to argue with her over-generalizations about men, which obviously included him. And besides, she must mean that she still loved him. "Louise, let me come to your cottage so we can discuss this face to face."

"No. Absolutely not." He could hear her take a deep breath before adding, "Justin, I'm not angry with you. Just disappointed. I had built up in my mind this foolish fantasy of you and I being married, partners in a unique medicine/healing arts office, probably in Dr. Clovis's mansion. Talk about! That's why I took your news so hard. But that doesn't mean I wish bad things for you. Concentrate on studying for your exams. After you pass them, as I'm sure you will, we can talk again."

"But—"

"It's the best way. We both need time to think. It's only another week."

He was afraid that, if he didn't resolve this now, her feelings toward him would be cemented. Too much thinking wouldn't help his case, he was sure.

"Look, Justin. Your tests are on September tenth and eleventh. Come see me after that. But don't contact me before that. I mean it, Justin. No phone calls, no visits, no letters. Nothing."

"All right. The train takes two days. So, I'll be back here on September fourteenth then," he said. "Okay?"

"Okay. Best wishes on your tests. I'll say a prayer for you."

Her words sounded so calm and positive, but Justin wasn't fooled. "I love you, Louise," he said again.

She didn't respond. In fact, he heard the click of the phone, then a dial tone.

CHAPTER 10

I'll walk alone...

*L*ouise went about her business for the next week with a heavy heart, but she was getting by.

This was unlike the time after Phillipe's death, the period when she'd suffered from what she called her Big Grief, when she'd been reduced to a zombie-like depression, combined with a period of wild, boozy, promiscuous behavior, until she'd learned of her pregnancy. Her mother had come to her aid then.

Ahem, the voice in her head said.

My mother and St. Jude, she corrected.

Thank you very much.

Did this mean that she didn't love Justin?

No, she definitely loved him.

As much as she'd loved Phillipe?

No.

Yes.

She couldn't decide.

Maybe it was just a different kind of love.

So, Louise went out onto the bayou to gather her herbs, and thought about Justin. And her heart hurt so bad....

Could I really live anywhere other than the bayou?

Maybe a day or two. Even a week. But more than that...I don't think I could breathe.

She took care of Adèle and listened to incessant questions about Justin. And her heart hurt so bad....

Tante Lulu, when will Justin come back?

Tante Lulu, is Justin mad at us?

Tante Lulu, why cain't we call Justin on the telephone?

Tante Lulu, could Justin mebbe be my daddy some day?

When she took her vegetables and fig jams into Boudreaux's to sell, she fielded questions from Justin's mother. And her heart hurt so bad....

Mrs. Boudreaux was being extra pleasant to her because she thought Louise might be in contact with her son or maybe because she pictured Louise as a future daughter-in-law. Louise was wary of Mrs. Boudreaux, ever since Justin had mentioned his mother's gossip about Adèle's family.

Have you heard from Justin?

Doan you look pretty in that straw hat.

Come, sit a spell so we kin talk.

Is that a new blouse? Very chic.

How's that niece of yours?

When she lay in bed at night, she couldn't help but replay in her head all the lovemaking that had taken place there. And it hurt so bad....

His kisses...oh, he is such a good kisser....

The way he smiles when he hears me moan....

The gasp he makes when I touch him there....

How I feel when he first enters me....

The bliss of being held afterward....

Louise didn't need a calendar to know that time was

ticking down, and before she knew it, it was the evening of September 13. Justin would be here tomorrow. And still she worried over certain essential issues. Whether or not she loved Justin was not in question; that was a given.

Could she live up north for a short period of time, let alone years?

Would Adèle suffer in such a confined space, in a poor neighborhood?

Could she sell her family cottage if it became necessary for them to afford a bigger apartment in Chicago, or to get Justin back here?

Did love overcome all these questions?

She thought and she thought and she thought. And her heart hurt so bad....

~

*I'll never smile again.... **On the other hand...***

Justin had taken his medical boards and was fairly certain he'd not only passed, but did so with flying colors, no thanks to Louise and his mind-numbing worries over what would happen with her. On the other hand, she'd said she would pray for him. So, maybe that had helped.

He'd cleared out a massive amount of stuff from his Boston apartment, but he hadn't needed to take any of the furnishings, which were pretty much yard sale finds, since a pal of his, Harry Olson, would continue with the lease. Heavy books, a medical bag and portable equipment, plus out-of-season clothing had been boxed up and were ready for transit. He'd left two sets of mailing labels with Harry to put on the boxes, only one of which would be used, after he gave him a call...either for Houma, Louisiana or for Chicago.

Now he was back in Louisiana and about to have his

big talk with Louisa. Unfortunately, after taking a bus to New Orleans and then to Houma, where he'd picked up his mother's car, and having to spend an hour showering, shaving, changing clothes, and then talking with his parents, it was almost nine p.m. before he'd got to Louise's cottage. By now, she probably thought he wasn't coming. Or maybe she didn't care.

Mon Dieu! He was anxious as a hooker at a Holy Roller convention.

He knocked on the door, and, when Louise answered, he saw that she'd dressed for company...for him? *Please, God!* She was wearing a short-sleeved, scoop-necked dress with big-ass, brightly-colored flowers—purple gardenias, yellow hibiscus, pink orchids, green ferns, and purple lilies, all on a pale blue background. Sort of Hawaiian-Cajun. (*I should have worn sunglasses. Ha, ha, ha!*) Glossy watermelon red lipstick (*I wonder if it tastes like watermelon. Ha, ha, ha!*) matched the toenails that could be seen in the peep-toe, white high heels she wore. (*For her, I could turn into one of those foot fetish perverts, maybe. Ha, ha, ha.*) Her hair was upswept and held in place with lacquer combs. (*The best part of those updo's, in a man's opinion, is taking them down, especially if it's a prelude to— Cut it out, Justin! You need to focus. Keep your cool. Stop wringing your hands with nervousness. Jeesh!*)

In any case, he interpreted the special care she'd taken with her appearance as a good sign, which was probably pathetic of him. For all he knew, she had a date with someone else, or had come back from an early date.

"Louise, darlin', I have missed you so much," he said, following her into the living room.

"I've missed you, too," she said, but the sad expression on her face did not bode well for him.

To hell with caution and taking things easy, as he'd

planned. He stepped forward and took her into his arms. Just hugging her. And kissing the top of her head. She felt so good. And she wasn't pushing him away. At first, anyway.

When she did begin to press her hands against his chest, he stepped back immediately and tilted his head in question. "Sweetheart…?"

"Let's sit down," she suggested, and motioned toward the davenport. In front of it, on a coffee table, were two stemmed glasses with a pale yellowish liquid in them. "And try my new batch of dandelion wine."

He waited for her to sit down before dropping down beside her. Not too close, but not too far away, either. He took his glass in hand and clinked it against the one she'd picked up. He wanted to say, "To us," but figured that would come off as presumptuous. Instead, he said, "To good wine." But then, after taking a sip, he added, "This is really good."

"Thank you. It did turn out well."

"Do you sell it?"

She shook her head. "No, that would be illegal. I just give it to friends. It makes an especially good addition to Christmas gift baskets, along with my jams and pickles and other homemade items." She was rambling. Maybe she was nervous, too. He wasn't sure if that was good or bad.

"You are incredible," he remarked and took another sip. Waving at the wine glasses and a plate of crackers and cheese (he wouldn't be surprised if she'd made those from scratch, too), he said, "So, you were expecting me this late? You're not dolled up for someone else?"

"Is that what you thought?" She straightened with affront.

Uh-oh! He shrugged. "I was afraid."

"Pfff! That doesn't say much about your opinion of me."

"No, it says more about my opinion of myself and whether I've shot my chances with you to hell. This week has been a nightmare for me, Louise." He took her hand in his.

She didn't pull away. "I haven't slept two hours straight all week."

He raised her hand and kissed the knuckles.

She did pull her hand away then and asked, "How did the tests go?"

"Good. I won't get the final results for a few days, but I'm certain I passed."

"Then you're Doctor Boudreaux now?"

"Pretty much."

"Congratulations. Of course, I knew you would do well."

"Oh, you did, did you?" He flicked her chin with a forefinger in a teasing manner. "And why was that? Your prayers to St. Jude?"

"Well, there was that," she said with a smile. "But I was talking to Leon when I went to deliver some produce a few days ago, and he told me that you are super, super intelligent. His words exactly. According to Leon, back when you were in high school, the students were given intelligence tests and your score went off the page."

"Leon said that?" He was surprised. Usually he and his brother only had fond insults for each other, never anything serious. He wondered about the context of any conversation in which that subject might come up.

"Yep, and then I met Dr. Clovis at church last Sunday and he told me that he knew one of your professors at Harvard, a colleague of his from way back. This guy told Dr. Clovis that you are a brilliant student and that he fully expects you to be a brilliant doctor someday. Dr. Clovis has pretty much accepted that you won't be joining his practice, your ambitions being much greater than his lowly practice."

"I wouldn't say that."

They were smiling at each other, but then Louise's expression changed as she took one of his hands in hers and said, "I've made a decision, Justin."

"Oh, no, no, no! You can't make a decision without us talking first." That look on her face was the kiss of death. Guys from the age of puberty to geezerhood knew the female expression that preceded the dumping. The only thing missing was the standard, "It's not you, it's me."

She started to say, "It's not—"

But he clamped a hand over her mouth to prevent the words from coming out. Which was silly. So, he removed his hand and stood abruptly, turning away from her so that she wouldn't see the tears that scalded his eyes. He blinked several times, then turned to face her.

She stood, too, but didn't move any closer. "Tell me the truth, Justin. Have you already accepted the Chicago offer?"

This was not the way he'd wanted, even rehearsed, this conversation going. But it was too late now. "Yes," he said, quickly adding, "But I've got a plan that will work out for all of us, I promise, even Adèle. I assume she's sleeping."

Louise nodded. "I'll listen, Justin, but I really have made up my mind."

"Don't tell me," he said in a panic. "Let me talk first."

"Okay," she said on a sigh that was not promising. She sat down again on the couch and patted the cushion for him to sit, as well.

He sat, and before beginning his spiel, he drank down the remainder of wine in his glass in one gulp, then did the same with what remained of Louise's.

She arched her brows at him, knowing he was not a

heavy drinker. "Justin! You're as nervous as a cat in a roomful of rocking chairs. You have nothing to be nervous about with me."

"I have everything to be nervous about with you," he disagreed. "I love you and can't imagine a life without you in it. I know we started out in agreement that this would be just an affair...a short one, but be honest, we both fell hard and fast."

She didn't disagree, but the determined expression on her face didn't soften either.

"Let's get one thing out of the way first. I don't give a hoot in hell's hollow whether Adèle is your daughter or your niece. I should have realized the bond between you two wouldn't withstand a separation of even a few weeks, let alone months or years. Blame it on pure male egotism, or selfishness, or just not thinking. But, sweetheart, the bond between you and me is just as strong. At least, it is from my end."

"Oh, Justin. This isn't about whether you love me or not. Can't you see—"

He put a forefinger to her lips to silence her. "Hear me out, sweetheart. I've been practicing this spiel all day. People on the two-day train ride from Boston probably thought I'd lost a few screws...or was just one of those crazy redneck Southerners."

She smiled, but only slightly.

"I phoned my contact at the hospital in Chicago and we had a long talk about my situation. He didn't think I would have any time outside my studies and residency to get a job to supplement my income so we could find better living arrangements, but he did say that the wives of some of the married residents got work in the hospital...offices, cafeteria, that kind of thing."

"And where would Adèle be when we were both working?"

"You could get hours while she's in school."

"Kindergarten is only half a day, Justin."

"I know that. I could also get a loan from my parents, though they're not wealthy by any means. Honey, I'm just trying to say that we, together, could find a way that would work for us. And it would only be temporary."

"Temporary to an adult is different than temporary to a child," she argued. "A month is like a year to a child. Three years would be like forever for Adèle. As for borrowing money from your parents, I would never do that. Never!"

"That was just an example. I would be a good risk for a bank loan."

"Pffff!"

"I'm trying to look at the bigger picture. In three years, I'll probably be able to name my salary. We would have more than enough in the long term to have a home in a good neighborhood, a family including more children if you want, two cars, a few luxuries. Wouldn't that be worth the sacrifice?"

"You're missing *my* bigger picture, Justin."

His heart sank. He was losing this battle.

"I've had a lot of time to think this week, and I've come to some conclusions." The sadness in her beautiful eyes crushed him with foreboding.

"Number one, I am a mother, and Adèle and what is best for her, comes first. Living in a city would not be good for her.

"Number two, like Adèle, living in a city would kill my soul. I didn't realize, until faced with the possibility of losing it, that the bayou is part of my identity. It's who I am. My heritage. The way I feel when I breathe in the bayou air. The plants and animals that give me sustenance.

"Number three, I am a *traiteur*. Folk healing is a gift passed down through all the female generations in my family. But I am specifically a bayou *traiteur*. My skills would not fit in a city setting.

"Number four, you are going to be an amazing doctor, but more than that. As a pioneer in a new specialty that you're already passionate about, I suspect you're destined for bigger things. Your ambition, tied with your gifts, might even make you famous. That's not going to happen here in Houma as a family doctor, which is something you offered to do for me. And, yes, I know there's nothing wrong with general practice, but not for you."

"Don't burn bridges you might want to cross someday, sweetheart."

"The bridge is already gone, Justin. I'm sorry."

"But—"

She shook her head. The tears which had been welling in her eyes spilled over and streamed down her face. She didn't even bother to swipe at them, even though she had to realize the tears were messing up her mascara, as well.

He used a thumb to swipe at one of the fat black tears and sighed, "Oh, sweetheart. It doesn't have to be this way."

"Let me finish while I still can," she said on a slight sob. She took both of his hands in hers. "It's over, Justin. It has to be. For your sake and for mine." He must have moaned because she squeezed his hands.

"Don't you love me anymore?" he asked over the lump in his throat the size of an orange. "Is that what this is about?"

She shook her head as tears continued to flow. "I love you, and I love the time we've had together. Most of all I have to thank you for bringing me out of my Big Grief over Phillipe. You helped me turn a corner that has blocked me for years."

"Great. I do all the work so some other guy can step in."
She slapped him playfully on the arm.

"I also have to thank you for helping me regain my Cajun Sass."

"Fuck Cajun Sass!"

"Tsk-tsk-tsk!" she said. It was a word he'd never used around her before. But she was smiling. Smiling through her tears.

"Maybe I can find some Chicago chick who needs to learn some Cajun Sass," he joked, though his heart was breaking. "I'm already handy with a syringe. Maybe I could inject a bit of tabasco in their veins." Tabasco was a Louisiana invention, infused into almost every dish.

She burst out laughing.

And that's how it ended. Tears and laughter.

～

AND THE BIG *Grief hits again...*

The next two weeks were hard for Louise. Of course they were. She was constantly breaking out in tears and blowing her nose. Adèle told more than one of Louise's customers who asked about her aunt's red eyes, "Tante Lulu has a head cold."

Didn't matter that Louise was the one who'd ended her relationship with Justin. She loved the man, and she missed him terribly. But their situation was hopeless and had to end. And, yes, she'd gone to St. Jude for help before and after her final meeting with Justin, but the saint had remained silent in her head. Louise took that to mean that Justin was not the one for her, not for the long term, not as her husband.

So, she had to move on. Complicating matters, or perhaps helping her by forcing routine activity, was Adèle;

Louise had to maintain a happy face or at least a normal face, even when inside she was screaming with pain. No lying in bed like a zombie, or running around to dive bars acting like a slut, or drinking herself into oblivion, all of which she'd done to some extent after Phillipe's death, until she realized she was pregnant.

Preparing for kindergarten occupied some of her time, buying school clothes and supplies. Taking Adèle to the dentist for her first check-up and to Dr. Clovis for her physical. Dr. Clovis said nothing about Justin, as if sensing her pain, and she loved him for that. Would a city doctor have that kind of compassion for a patient? Would he even know her well enough to be aware of a heartbreak?

As the weeks passed, she harvested her fall vegetables and brought them to Boudreaux's store for sale. She managed to avoid talking with his family about Justin's current circumstances in Chicago. It was for the best that she stifled any urges to inquire about how he was doing. She would have to find some other outlet for her produce. Or increase her *traiteur* business which was flourishing, and stop growing so darn many fruits and vegetables.

Louise realized several things as she began to heal. She hadn't loved Justin as much as she'd loved Phillipe. She would never get over Phillipe until she met him again in heaven. But Justin…well, she did love him. Perhaps she always would in some distant way. She did not want to diminish or negate the power of the feelings they had shared. However, slowly but surely, he was becoming a memory…a good memory. Poignant, but good. While she'd labeled her constant sorrow after Phillipe as her Big Grief, she figured her current sorrow amounted to Big-But-Survivable Grief. She would have followed Phillipe to the ends of the earth. She hadn't been willing to follow Justin beyond Louisiana. That said something, didn't it?

She had one big thing to thank Justin for. He'd somehow managed to kickstart her Cajun Sass back in place. And good thing, too, because some of the bayou folks who frequented the rumor mill had become very judgmental. Not all of them, but enough to be noticeable. Not knowing the whole story...whether she'd engaged in illicit sexual activity, or whether she'd dumped Justin, or vice versa, or just because she was a single woman living alone out there on the bayou where "who knew what" could go on...they gave her the snooty treatment, including Leon's wife, Lily Rose, who was several months pregnant and proud of it, as if she was the first woman alive to get preggers. Lily Rose probably resented the fact that Louise had never made an appointment in her salon.

The last time Louise was in the store, Lily Rose approached her and said, "Louise, Louise, you poor dear. Workin' out there in the swamps with those smelly ol' plants. Pee-you!" She sniffed the air as if Louise smelled bad. "How does it feel to lose yer last chance fer catchin' a husband? Maybe you need a new hairdo, or somethin', bless yer heart."

Louise put her hands on her hips and stared Lily Rose in her heavily made-up face before drawling out, "Frankly, my dear Lily Rose, you can kiss my go-to-hell." Every woman in the South had seen *Gone With the Wind* at least two times and knew that famous "Frankly, my dear" line by heart.

"Well, I never," Lily Rose said on a gasp.

"Ain't that the truth, honey?" Louise replied, shaking her head as if Lily Rose was a pitiful soul, which she was.

"Rumor sez that you—" Lily Rose started to say.

Rumor sez that," Louise interrupted, not wanting to know what people were saying about her, "before you 'caught' yer husband Leon, you'd seen more ceilings than Michelangelo."

It took Lily Rose several moments to get the insult and she gasped, "Oh…oh…!"

On that note, Louise pivoted and stormed out of the store and drove to town. Once in Houma, she had her hair cut and permed at that new salon on the corner into a curly bob that made her look…sassy. The next day, still fuming from her encounter with Lily Rose, Louise went shopping and came away with three sets of nylons, a pair of strappy high heels, two silk blouses, a pair of hiney-hugging pants, and a new wraparound dress, all in bright *sassy* colors. The third day, she picked up Adèle from her morning kindergarten session.

"Where we going, auntie?" Adèle asked when she noticed them going in the opposite direction from home.

"It's a surprise," Louise said and drove a short distance before driving into a used car lot on the outskirts of Houma. Dapper Dan's. Dan had mentioned at the wedding reception last month that he could give her a good deal on a trade-in. Adèle skipped along beside her and Dan as they walked up one aisle and down another before exclaiming with joy, "Look, Tante Lulu, it's a purple car."

"Well, butter mah butt an' call me a biscuit," Louise muttered under her breath.

It was actually lavender, not purple, which was Adèle's favorite color, and it was a convertible, but it was big…a Chevy Impala.

"Oh, I doan know," Dan protested. "It's kinda big for a little ol' gal like you. You'd need a pillow or two so you could see over the dashboard."

It was crazy. Impractical. But it sure would make a statement.

A short time later, with cushions under both their

behinds, Louise and Adèle grinned at each other as they drove off the lot in the new Lillian.

If this isn't Cajun Sass, nothing is, Louise thought.

To her surprise, the voice was back in her head, and he proclaimed, *'Tis the best cure for hopelessness.*

The car?

No, my child. The attitude...the Cajun Sass.

Louise never lost her Cajun Sass after that. In fact, she grew an attitude that became legendary.

CHAPTER 11

Present day

As time goes by...

*L*ouise sat in the passenger seat of Luc's ess-you-vee as they drove to the Triple L Ranch for the big birthday bash. They were a little late because Louise had insisted on extra precautions being made with the Peachy Praline Cobbler Cake she'd brought.

Not that there wouldn't be a birthday cake there already, but knowing Charmaine, it would probably be store-bought, and everyone knew they were never as good as homemade, even if it came from Samantha's upscale family supermarket chain, Starr Foods. Samantha was married to Dr. Daniel LeDeux, one of Louise's many "great-nephews." Their sons, the D & A twins, were among the seven birthday boys today, even though they were six months older.

Tee-John's wife, Sylvie, sat in the back with their one-year-old son Christopher, who was asleep in his car seat.

Good thing, too. Chris was one of the birthday boys, and he would need all his energy to keep up with his cousins who looked like a marathon of crawlers when they were all together. She wouldn't be surprised if some of them started walking today as they tried to imitate D & A who'd recently discovered toddling, amidst lots of spills on their diaper-padded bottoms. If they didn't start walking soon, Louise intended to make them knee pads.

"I still don't see why you had to bring your car, too," Luc said. "Lillian is a gas guzzler. You oughta get rid of that thing."

"As if!" she replied, glancing behind to see that her lavender convertible was indeed riding their tail. They had all been surprised when their family arrived to pick up Louise and she'd asked Luc's three daughters if one of them could drive her car to the ranch. The three girls had all practically jumped with glee. The oldest, Blanche, 20, who was following in her daddy's footsteps as a law student at Tulane, won out as the driver. Camille, 19, a French Quarter chef in training, rode shotgun; and a disgruntled Jeanette, about to be a high school senior, sat in back.

"I have my reasons for wanting Lillian at the ranch," Louise told Luc then, but not feeling obliged to explain herself. "Speaking of gas guzzlers, what were you thinkin' when you bought that boat las' month? I hear tell it's like a mini yacht. You havin' a mid-life crisis or somethin'?"

Sylvie giggled from the back seat and said, "That's putting him in his place, Tante Lulu."

"It's a fishing boat."

"What? You cain't buy yer fish from Captain B.J.'s market lak everyone else? Or throw a line in the bayou?"

"Hmfph! Arguing with you is lak throwing sticky rice against the wall," Luc said, but he was grinning. He loved arguing with her, and they both knew it. "I sure hope you don't think I'll allow you to drive back yourself tonight."

"I sure hope you don't think you're the boss of me," she replied.

He rolled his eyes, which was the usual reaction from her great-nephews (or grandsons, if they only knew) when she said something they disagreed with. A bunch of know-it-alls, they were, bless their hearts.

"Did you hear Dad is in the hospital again? Pretty bad shape this time."

"Valcour?"

"He's the only Dad I have. Unfortunately."

"His liver, I bet. The human body kin take only so much booze…and meanness." Louise didn't usually wish ill on folks, but Valcour LeDeux had been her sworn enemy ever since he'd ruined Adèle's life and a whole passel of legitimate and illegitimate children he begat on dozens of women throughout the South. Luc understood better than most why she hated the man so. After Adèle suffered years of abuse following her marriage to the brute when she was only seventeen, she died of cancer (though Louise was inclined to attribute it to heartbreak). She left behind three pitiful orphan boys, Luc being the oldest at twelve, followed by Rene and Remy, who'd been only nine and eight. Luc had done his best in the rusted-out trailer they called home, trying to care for his younger brothers, including washing their clothes for school in a nearby stream when the washing machine broke down or the power was turned off for failure to pay the electric bill. Many a time, one or all the boys would flee to her cottage for protection. The authorities would do nothing in those days because Valcour was the father.

Years later, oil was discovered on Valcour's property, and he became a wealthy man, in cahoots with the petroleum companies that raped the bayou. He married again and had Tee-John, but he still spread his seed from one end of the state to the other. At last count, Louise figured he had fathered at least fifteen legitimate and illegitimate kids. And Louise, though blood related to only three of them, had become Tante Lulu to them all. In fact, to everyone on the bayou. Not a bad legacy, she figured.

Still, if Valcour was dying or something, he would get his just desserts on the other side. It wasn't her place to judge. "I'm sorry, Luc. He's yer daddy, no matter what," she said. "Do ya think I should go visit him?"

"Whaaat?" Luc exclaimed and glanced her way with horror. "Don't you dare. He'd probably have a heart attack, on top of everything else."

"Whatever you say," she replied, folding her hands with innocence on her lap. *At least I tried. Maybe I'll go see him anyhow.*

They were approaching the gates to Triple L Ranch now. By the looks of all the vehicles parked in front of the rustic lodge style home and in a nearby pasture, they were among the last to arrive. And there were numerous newspaper and TV vans with those dishes on top parked outside the fence.

She assumed that they were here for her great-great-"nephew" (or great-grandson) who supposedly planned to make some kind of announcement about his football career plans any day now. Even though they weren't here for her, you never knew when you might catch the cameraman's eye. Therefore, Louise was glad she'd dressed in her most photogenic outfit—a red-and-white polka dot, wraparound sundress with matching red, low-heeled sandals (not her favorite red high heels on a property where horse poop might pop up at any moment), and a straw sun hat with pretty red roses. Her lipstick and nail and toe polish were matching shades of "Hot Sex" from Charmaine's salon. Not that she'd had any of that for a long, long time. *Not with a partner, ha, ha, ha.* After changing her mind over and over, she'd finally settled on her strawberry blonde Reba McEntire wig in a shoulder-length bouncy style that fitted her mood today.

"Welcome, everyone!" said Raoul Lanier, or Rusty as he was known, who came down the wide front steps of the big, rambling log home they referred to as a "lodge" to greet them. He waved at Sylvie who was just getting out of the car and said, "And happy birthday to you, young Christopher."

Chris was still half asleep in his mother's arms, his head resting on her shoulder, a thumb locked in his tiny mouth, but he gave Rusty a shy smile.

Rusty was around fifty years old, but he was still the hottest Cajun in Louisiana. And that was saying a lot. All the LeDeux males were good looking, and Cajun men in general had what girls in her day called the va-va-voom factor. But with Rusty...well, women did double takes when he walked down the street, especially if he was wearing his cowboy hat and tight jeans. Whoo-ee! She had to give the man credit, though; he had eyes only for Charmaine. Even after all these years, his eyes lit up when she walked into a room (usually with a sexy swish of her hips) and he was wont to mutter his usual expression, "Mercy!"

Sylvie went into the house with Chris, mentioning something about needing a bathroom. Rusty leaned down and gave Louise a warm hug, followed by a full-body perusal and a wolf whistle. "You're lookin' good today, Tante Lulu."

Louise wasn't sure if he was serious or poking fun at her. Didn't matter. She dressed for herself, not anyone else.

"Kin you help Luc with mah cake? Mebbe you should put it in the fridge fer a while. It might melt in this heat."

Rusty's attention was drawn then to Luc, who was swearing under his breath (*as if I can't hear him*) as he tried to maneuver her unwieldy cake out of the car; it must weigh about ten pounds.

"We don't have a fridge that big," Rusty said.

"Put it in one of yer cow trucks then."

"My cow trucks?" Rusty looked at Luc who had pulled the cake on its three-foot tray onto the tailgate of his SUV.

Luc shrugged at Rusty. "She probably means one of those refrigerated meat trucks."

Why were people always trying to interpret what she said? As if she spoke another language. Idjits, that's what they were!

Rusty looked back at her. "I don't have refrigerated meat trucks. My cows are alive when we truck them to market."

Louise waved a hand airily. "Whatever. I smell cow."

"Of course you smell cow. This is a cattle ranch."

"Doan be snippy with me. I meant cooked cow."

"Oh. Sorry. The firepits were just opened, and the meat is resting."

"Come out on the patio, auntie," Charmaine said. She'd just come out of the front door and onto the porch. "Everyone's here, waitin' fer you so the party can start."

Louise didn't doubt that one bit. "Where's Timmy?"

"I just put him down for a nap. He's been crawling around like a crazy bedbug all morning."

Charmaine came down the steps and hugged Louise. "You look wonderful today, auntie," she said.

Rusty and Luc looked at her like she must be blind, or was seeing something they didn't.

But then, Charmaine was dressed in a strapless little

hot pink sundress that molded her body on top and swirled out in a bunch of pleats to mid-thigh. On her feet were high-heeled wedgie sandals, which, combined with her already tall frame, made her about six feet tall. Her hair was a mass of spiral curls. Her make-up was perfect. And huge chandelier earrings dangled all the way to her shoulders. Since she'd begun nursing her baby and still did occasionally, her breasts, already a buxom 34C, had blossomed out to porno fullness. In her strapless dress made of some light cotton material, the shape of the enlarged nipples was clearly visible.

"Girl, be careful we doan get any breezes t'day, or yer gonna get old and new-monia in that outfit. Tee, hee, hee," Louise said.

Rusty gaped as Charmaine approached him and said, clear as a bell, "Mercy!"

Luc, who was Charmaine's half-brother, said, "I am not looking. I am not looking."

Honestly, Charmaine had Cajun Sass down to an art form. It still puzzled Louise why Mary Lou went to someone as old as her and not to Charmaine for advice. But then, she recalled that Mary Lou had mentioned how embarrassing it would be to confide in her mother.

Which reminded Louise...it was her goal today to see just how well Mary Lou was doing in her Cajun Sass lessons. Looking for her, she looped arms with Charmaine and walked around the side of the house to the back yard, then came to a screeching halt.

There had to be at least seventy-five people standing around the firepit, sitting on folding chairs on the grass and at umbrella tables on the flagstone patio. A bunch of toddlers and young'uns had been plopped inside a twenty-foot wide portable fence, which pretty much amounted to an outdoor playpen.

Laughter and splashing noises came from the other side of the house where there was an in-ground swimming pool.

"Lawdy, lawdy, didja invite everyone in the parish?"

Charmaine laughed. "Nope. You gotta realize, auntie, that we have more than fifty in our immediate family alone. No thanks to you."

"I keep tellin' you, I had nothin' to do with all you gals getting' preggers las' year. All I did was say that I wished there were more babies around."

"Yeah, well, don't be doin' any wishin' t'day."

Louise just grinned. Let them all think she had that kind of power.

Someone came from behind and put hands over her eyes. "Guess who?"

She smelled coconut sunscreen and recognized the voice. "Lak I wouldn't know you anywhere, Etienne LeDeux," she said, turning around and straightening her hat to give Tee-John's oldest a fake glare.

He gave her cheek a quick kiss and danced away from her as she attempted to swat him on the arm with her St. Jude fan. What a rascal, just like his Papa was. He was only fourteen years old, but his thin body, already almost six foot tall, in a wet bathing suit and nothing else, showed promise of a hunkiness that would have the girls buzzin' around him like bees to honey.

"I tol' ya, Tante Lulu, that I changed mah name ta Steve," the boy, who was fourteen going on forty, said and grinned at her. "My name's too hard fer mah friends ta pronounce."

Steven was the English translation of Etienne.

"Why's it so hard ta say Ay-T-en? Yer friends mus' be dumb as stumps."

Etienne just laughed and hugged her to his side. Never

mind that he was wet. She didn't care. She loved the boy, almost as much as she did his daddy.

René came up to them then, on his way to a small wooden platform that had been set up over near the barbecue pits. He wore a black tank top, khaki shorts, flip-flops and a baseball cap on his head with the logo "Swamp Rats," which was the name of the band he played with on weekends when he wasn't teaching school. He had a *frottir*, or washboard, hung over his shoulders.

"Oh, goody, we're gonna have music," she said, clapping her hands. "This party is lookin' kinda...boring." Her eyes widened with surprise as she hit on that word. *Maybe Mary Lou isn't the only one needing sassed up with Cajuness.*

"Would it be a *fais do do*, a party on the bayou, if there was no music? René asked.

"Speakin' of boring...it occurs ta me, René, that we haven't done our Cajun Village People act in ages. Isn't it time to resurrect our group?" Louise asked.

René let out a little hoot of laughter and several men standing nearby, who'd overheard their conversation—Luc, Remy, and Rusty—gave her dirty looks and said, as one, "No way!" One of them even added, "No frickin' way!"

"What's the Village People?" Etienne wanted to know.

"The Village People were a campy type of disco music group in the 1970s, all men, known for their costumes... cowboy, cop, construction worker, soldier, biker, that kind of thing," René explained.

"And they did a sexy kind of dance while they sang," Louise contributed, "sort of like the Chippendudes." She fanned herself as if she got hot just thinking about them.

"Eew!" René said.

She swatted him with her purse, which was about the size of a boat.

While Etienne was pulling a little Ziplock bag out of

his back pocket which held a phone and was then tapping in some buttons, Louise elaborated, "For a while back there, we formed the Cajun Village People, made up of all the men in the family when they wanted to woo a young gall who was havin' none of them. Sort of a serenading."

"Strippers?" exclaimed Jude LeDeux, René's son, who had walked up to see what was going on. Jude was only ten years old, but looked a lot like his father. Another hunk-to-be. "Whoa, Dad! You and the uncles were strippers? Cool!"

"Us wimmen were involved, too. I think I still have mah red spandex dress. I could pull it out, easy peasy."

René make a choking sound which he tried to hide as a cough. Then he told Etienne and his son, "The Village People were not strippers. They just had moves that some people considered…um, suggestive. They only had a couple of hits before they broke up. 'YMCA' and 'Macho Man', as I recall."

All of a sudden, "'Macho Man' blared out of Etienne's phone, and he went bug-eyed at whatever he was seeing on the screen before remarking, "Cool! I could do that. Mebbe I could be Steve the Surfer Dude." Then he yelled out to one of his cousins, "Hey, Mike, wanna be in the new Cajun Village People?"

Male heads around the yard shot up with alarm at those words and the music.

But then Mary Lou showed up, finally. She had been off on a trail ride with her cousin Andy and a new hotshot recruit for the New Orleans Saints, Bobby Jones, affectionately known as "Happy Legs" because of his fast strides on the football field. After the introduction, while she and Mary Lou watched the two men walk off to get a beer, Louise remarked to Mary Lou, "Looks to me lak he's got a Happy Hiney, too."

"Tante Lulu!" Mary Lou chided her with a laugh. "But, yeah, that is one very fine butt."

"Shh! It's okay if an old lady lak me sez that, but it's sexual harassment if you do."

Mary Lou pretended to zip her mouth.

Louise stepped away from Mary Lou then to give her a better look. Head to toe and back up again.

Mary Lou did a little spin to show off her new look, grinning like a cabbage-eating skunk. "What do you think, auntie?"

"Seems ta me, mah work is done. You got Cajun Sass down jist right."

Mary Lou wore jeans, but they were white and tight and hung low on her hips, leaving a good six inches of skin exposed up to the cropped top of a blue spandex top, under which she had to be wearing one of them push-up or pump-me-up type bras because she sure wasn't that buxom last week. Good for her! And wait…was that a tiny gold ring winking in her belly button? If Louise was younger, she thought she might try one of those. But that wasn't everything. The girl must have gotten a haircut from her mother because it was shoulder-length now and curly, too short for one of her usual ponytails. She didn't wear much make-up, but there was a hint of rosy lip gloss.

"And it feels good, too," Mary Lou said, still grinning.

The two of them dropped down to a bench and continued talking.

"That dumb Derek won't be callin' you boring now, thass fer sure."

"I already know that."

Louise arched her brows at the girl.

"He was here earlier. Yeah, I know, he has some nerve showing up at the ranch. It was obvious he was still wanting to run into Andy. But he took one look at me and about swallowed his tongue. Tried to take back what he'd said about me being boring and denied that he'd dumped me."

"What did you say?"

"I said, 'Hit the road, Derek. Yer much too boring fer a sexy girl like me.'"

"Good!" Louise said, clapping a hand on her knee.

"Also, he about turned green when I mentioned that the new Saints player, Happy Legs Jones, asked me for a date. Horseback riding!"

Louise laughed. "I almost forgot. I have somethin' fer you. C'mon." She got up and started to walk around the house, headed toward the pasture where all the cars were parked by now.

Hurrying to catch up, Mary Lou said, "Let me carry that for you."

Louise still had her purse in hand. She'd been about to go inside to the bathroom and touch up her make-up. It was probably worn off from all that cheek kissing she'd been doing since she arrived.

She handed the bag to Mary Lou, who pretended to stagger. "What do you have in here?"

"Everything. You know me, I'm allus prepared."

When they got to the pasture, which wasn't very far away, Louise finally saw where Lillian had been parked. Not hard to locate since it was the only lavender convertible in a sea of Ess-You-Vees and pick-up trucks.

Mary Lou frowned at her. "What's up? Do you want to go home? Oh, my God! Are you sick?"

"No, no. I'm okay." She put her purse on the back trunk area of the car and searched for the car keys, which, like always happened, were at the bottom. But first, she took out a cosmetic bag, a brush, a mirror, a canister of bug spray, a jar of her gator aloe salve, a pistol, a grocery list, her St. Jude fan, a handkerchief, a nail file, a rosary, and sunglasses. "Here," she said, handing the keys to Mary Lou. "This should be the final touch to yer Cajun Sass, honey."

Mary Lou frowned. "I don't understand."

"It's yours."

"What's mine?"

"The car. Lillian."

"What? For real?"

"Unless you doan want it."

"Oh, my God! Mine? Oh, my God!" she squealed. "I love it. I've always loved it."

She opened the driver's door and sat behind the wheel, touching the dashboard, fiddling with the knobs on the radio.

"It is awful big. Mebbe you'd rather have somethin' smaller."

"No, this is perfect. In fact, I bet I could hitch a horse trailer on this baby. I'm thinkin' about doing some rodeos. Barrel racing. Team roping. Pole bending."

"There you go," Louise said.

"But what are you gonna do for a car?" Mary Lou asked. "Maybe you need to rethink this."

Louise could tell that she didn't really want her to rescind the gift. "Actually, I have my eye on a little vintage Volkswagen convertible that's been restored in a pretty shade of glittery purple. Iridescent Grape, they call it. It'll be the new Lillian."

"Sounds perfect."

As they started to walk back toward the house, Mary Lou kept her longer strides in pace with Louise's much shorter ones, but Louise could tell that the girl wanted to run off to tell her parents and friends about her windfall. So, when they got to the porch, Louise told her to go ahead, alone, that she would follow later.

"Are you sure? I can stay with you."

"No. You go on. I'm gonna sit on the front porch for a while. All those people and all that noise are fine, but I need to take a break now and then."

The girl gave her a big hug, thanking her profusely. Once Louise was seated on one of the low rockers, Mary Lou was off with a whoop.

With a sigh, Louise rocked back and forth. She could hear music coming from the back of the house, along with laughter and muted voices. They could go on without her. Someday, probably sooner than later, they would have to. It wasn't that she didn't love a party, and she for sure loved her family, every single one of them, but she cherished her moments of solitude when she could grab them, too.

It was times like these when she thought of Phillipe. Yes, there had been other men in her life after Phillipe. Even ones she had loved. When she'd gotten too lonely, there had always been some man to step into her life. Like Justin, the doctor, who'd been the first. And so many others.

Still...*always*...she wondered what her life would have been like if Phillipe had survived the war. They would have married, of course. And had Adèle. Probably, they couldn't have prevented the cancer that took her at such a young age, but they might have, together, convinced their daughter not to become involved with that devil Valcour LeDeux.

On the other hand, she had to admit that Valcour made wonderful children. There wasn't a one of them that turned out bad, as far as she knew. And good-looking, too. The males and females, both, were stunners.

And here came one of the stunners now.

Tee-John sank down into the rocker next to her and sighed.

"Before you say anything, I'm fine. Jist restin' fer a bit."

"They'll be singin' happy birthdays and blowin' out the candles soon," he told her.

"I'll go back in a minute."

"I don't blame you for hidin' out here."

"I am not hidin' out. Cain't a gal jist rest? *By herself?*"

Tee-John didn't take the hint, his butt planted firmly in his rocker. And of course he had to talk, too. "It's a madhouse out there." They both rocked in comfortable silence for a few moments before Tee-John chuckled. "You created a real war zone, darlin'."

"How's that?"

"Giving Mary Lou your car. No one was expecting that. Now all the cousins are arguin' over what must be in store for them if yer startin' ta dole out yer belongings. What next? You orderin' yer coffin from Amazon, or somethin'? Kin I expect ta see it on yer back porch next time I come by?"

"Doan be silly." Actually, she didn't know you could order coffins off the Internet. She'd have to check into that.

"Etienne is convinced you must have a Lamborghini or an airplane in store fer him if Mary Lou got Lillian. Jude mentioned a motorcycle. Camille and Blanche are arguin' over yer cottage."

Louise shrugged. "They'll all get their due in time."

"And, *mon Dieu!* What's this I hear about you buying a VW?"

She shrugged again.

"You know it's time to give up driving."

Another shrug.

"You have heard of Uber, haven't you?"

"Fer goodness sake, Tee-John! I'm not dyin'. All I did was give a girl a gift ta boost her Cajun Sass. Thass all. You and yer brothers and sisters need ta find somethin' ta occupy yer time, instead of meddlin' in mah life."

"Meddling? Meddling?" he sputtered. "Yer the queen of meddling."

"Mebbe I should be makin' a wish or two," she said, narrowing her eyes at him, then grinning.

"Don't you dare!" he said, pretending to duck her evil eye.

"Well, mebbe we do have enough babies fer now. But surely it's time fer some matchmakin'. Doan we have some twenty-somethin's in the family what need a boost toward the altar?"

"Oh, my God!" Tee-John muttered.

Just then a vehicle pulled through the gate and drove right up to the front of the porch. It was a white van with the logo "Starr Foods" on the side.

"Oh, goody! It's mah date. I was afraid he took a nap and forgot ta come."

"A…a date?" Tee-John sputtered, then grinned, "Well, slap mah head and call me silly."

She slapped Tee-John on the arm to shush his silliness as she creakily rose from the rocker, then headed toward the dapper gentleman who exited the van. Tee-John stood, too, probably thinking she needed help down the steps.

It was Samuel Starr, Samantha's grandfather, the founder of the Starr Foods supermarket chain. He was dressed as usual, in a white suit, white shoes, planter's hat, and gray beard and mustache trimmed to perfection. Like the original Colonel Sanders, but better.

"Doan he look sexier than a hoot owl in them red suspenders?" she whispered to Tee-John. "Talk about!"

Tee-John made a sound halfway between a laugh and a snort.

"Hey, Sam! Yer jist in time fer the birthday cake 'n' singin'," Louise called out.

"Great," he said, taking two shopping bags filled with wrapped gifts from the back of the van.

"Ya doan hafta worry about how I'll get home t'night," Louise told Tee-John. "Sam will be takin' me home and..." She let her words trail off just to tease Tee-John whose jaw had dropped open.

But then Tee-John took her into a big hug which lifted her off her feet and caused her hat to fall off. Chuckling, he said into her ear, "You never change, do you, old lady?"

"Who you callin' an old lady?"

"You. One of these days you'll have to admit to being old."

"Hmpfh! Well, I may be old, but I ain't dead yet. I got lots ta do before I go to my glory."

"That's what I'm afraid of."

READER LETTER

Dear Readers:

Well, what did you think of the second prequel of Tante Lulu's history, following on WHEN LULU WAS HOT? These books are leading up to her senior years, when she first appeared in my Cajun series starting with THE LOVE POTION. Then she went sashaying with her eccentric and outrageous antics through twelve full-length novels to CAJUN PERSUASION? Whew! I never thought when I first started writing these stories that they would go on for so long, or that Tante Lulu would become such a beloved figure, bless her heart.

There should be at least one or two more of these long novella prequels, the next one taking us to Adèle as a teenager and young bride to Valcour LeDeux. And we need to find out when Tante Lulu started hearing the "thunderbolt of love" or making hope chests for all the men in her family or developing a passion for exercise guru Richard Simmons. After that, well, my goodness, there are lots of other stories in this LeDeux family to be told. Etienne, the quintessential rogue, once he's grown up. Rashid, the musician. Andy, the football player. Blanche, the lawyer. Camille, the chef. And so on.

Of course, I can't ignore my Vikings or Navy SEALS. I expect to return next to THE CAGED VIKING.

I took poetic license in a couple of places. For example, the Hank Williams' song "Jambalaya" came out in 1952, not 1951, the Terrebonne General Medical Center was actually established in 1954, not 1951, and *Rebel Without a Cause* came out in 1955, not 1951.

I love to hear from you readers. For more information, you can sign up for my newsletter on my website at *www. sandrahill.com*, or check out my Facebook page at Sandra-HillAuthor.

As always, I wish you smiles in your reading.

Sandra Hill

TANTE LULU'S PEACHY PRALINE COBBLER CAKE

The cake:

- white cake mix
- 3 whole eggs
- 1/3 cup oil
- 1 cup water

The streusel:

- 1/2 cup brown sugar (more or less, depending on taste)
- 2 pkgs (1.23 oz each) peaches and cream instant oatmeal
- 2 1.5 oz. pecan pralines, chopped (reserve 2 tbsp for garnish)
- 1/4 cup (1/2 stick) butter, melted

Fruit:

- 1 medium peach, sliced thin, or 1 small can peaches, thoroughly drained

The frosting:

- 1 cup milk
- 4 tbsp cornstarch
- 1/2 cup butter
- 1/2 cup Crisco
- 2 cups granulated sugar
- pinch of salt
- 2 tsp vanilla

The cake: Preheat oven to 350 degrees. Make cake batter and put into two round greased and floured cake pans. Mix streusel and sprinkle over top of both cakes. Bake 35 minutes or until toothpick inserted in center comes out clean. Let cakes cool.

The frosting: Cook milk and cornstarch until thick, stirring often. Cool. Cream all remaining ingredients, adding the cornstarch mixture gradually. It should be fluffy and not overly sweet.

Place one of the cooled layers, streusel side up, on a cake platter. Frost, topping with half the sliced peaches. Cover with the second cake, streusel side up. Frost top and sides. Garnish with sliced peaches in a pinwheel pattern, finishing with sprinkle of remaining chopped pralines.

Notes:

- This is a very rich cake because of the streusel

and instant oatmeal. If using plain oatmeal, the amount of brown sugar can be altered, to taste.

- Peach juice, if available, can be substituted for some or all of the water in the cake.
- Any white frosting can be used, keeping in mind how sweet the cake already is. A Crisco frosting (which can be found anywhere on the Internet) tends to be less sweet, which some people like.
- Of course, the white cake can be made from scratch.

Last bit of instructions from Tante Lulu: "Set out a pitcher of sweet tea, *chère*. Invite over your friends and family. Then, *laissez les bon temp rouler!* Let the good times roll!"

EXCERPT FROM WHEN LULU WAS HOT

Present Day
Sentimental Journey...

Louise Rivard, best known up and down the bayou as Tante Lulu, was celebrating her ninetieth birthday. For the second year in a row.

Or was it the third?

Maybe the fourth.

Whatever! she thought. *Age is just a number, like I always say. Some fools are old fogies at fifty, like rusted-out jalopies, bless their hearts, creepin' along the highway of life. Me, on the other hand, I still have a bucket-load of va-voom under my hood, and miles to go before I bite the dust.*

Bucket-load, bucket list, get it?

Ha, ha, ha! There's a hole in my bucket, there's a hole in my bucket...

Talking to herself was nothing new for Louise. Answering herself was another matter, especially when she answered in song. And, no, it had nothing to do with her age or that alls-hammer some seniors got. It was just that sometimes she was more fun than the people around her; so, she had to amuse herself.

Anyways, like she told her niece Charmaine last week, "Ninety is the new seventy."

"If that's true, then forty is the new twenty. Hal-le-lu-jah! Heck, I'll settle fer thirty." Charmaine, ever conscious of her age and appearance, had done a little boogie dance around Louise's kitchen to celebrate. "Maybe I'll have T-shirts made up fer mah beauty spas with that message. 'Forty Is the New Thirty' on the front, and on the back, 'And We Can Help. Cut & Die Hair Salon, Houma, Louisiana.'"

Charmaine owned a string of hair salons and beauty spas in Southern Louisiana. A self-proclaimed bimbo with a brain, she was always looking out for the main chance.

Which isn't a bad thing, necessarily, in my opinion.

Actually, Louise's birthday had already passed, and been celebrated in grand style with a pool party at her nephew Luc's house. Even so, today her LeDeux great-nephews and -nieces, along with a few great-greats, were treating her to a belated gift, some kind of secret destina-tion road trip. There were so many of the family tagging along that they were a highway caravan. Pick-up trucks, expensive sedans like Luc's BMW, even Louise's vintage, lavender Chevy Impala convertible, named Lillian, being driven by her great-great-niece Mary Lou, who was constantly pleading for first dibs on the vehicle in Louise's will.

To which, Louise always answered, "I ain't dead yet, girl. Mebbe I'll get buried in it, 'stead of some boring wood casket. Wouldn't that shock St. Peter if I came roarin' through the Pearly Gates? Not to worry. St. Jude would be out front, wavin' me in."

St. Jude was Louise's favorite go-to saint, the patron of

hopeless cases. And, whoo-boy, had she run into a passel of hopeless folks in her time! Herself included, especially after...well, a long time ago.

Louise was riding shotgun in the first vehicle, an SUV driven by her youngest LeDeux nephew, Tee-John, "tee-" being a Cajun prefix for small or little. Not so young anymore, Tee-John, a cop from up Lafayette way, was what modern people called thirty-something. And he was far from little anymore, either.

Tee-John's wife Celine sat in the back seat with their son, Etienne, who was thirteen going on twenty, a rascal just like his daddy had been...and probably still was. Lately, Etienne insisted that his friends call him by the English version of his name, Steven. If Louise heard, "Call me Steve," one more time when she talked to him, she was going to pitch a hissy fit.

"Ay-T-en is a perfectly good Cajun name, and you're Cajun ta the bone, boy," she often told him.

The rascal usually winked at her and said with an exaggerated drawl, "Ah know, auntie. Cantcha tell, ah got mah Cajun on all the time, guar-an-teed!"

As a contrast to their older brother, six- and five-year-old Annie and Rob were in the way-back seat, deaf to their surroundings with headsets connected to games on their cell phones. Etienne was expertly thumbing his way on his own phone, too, even as he talked. A multitasker!

What was the world coming to when children needed their own phones? Knowing Etienne, he was probably looking at nekkid pictures, or sending ones of himself. Lordy, Lordy, the boy was a trial. Girls up and down the bayou best beware when this boy got old enough to really get his Cajun on.

"Do you wanna know what yer surprise birthday gift is, auntie?" Tee-John asked her, once they were on the road.

"No, I wanna sit on my hiney playin' twenty questions," she griped. A trip to Baton Rouge was not her idea of fun, even if they went to some fancy pancy restaurant, or visited some historic site, or something else her family had in mind, like they usually did. She'd rather be working in her garden (she had two bushels of figs ready to be picked), or practicing her belly dancing (there was a competition coming up soon that she was thinking about entering), or playing bingo at Our Lady of the Bayou Church hall (where the jackpot this week was a Crock-Pot big enough to hold a small pig).

Ooh, ooh, ooh, an idea suddenly came to her. "Is Richard Simmons in town? Am I finally gonna meet my crush?" Since the exercise guru had disappeared from the public eye in recent years, she'd been worried about him.

Tee-John rolled his eyes, and she heard snickering from Celine. "Who's Richard Simmons?" Call-me-Steve asked.

She shook her head with disgust. No one understood her longtime fascination with the exercise celebrity. She knew Richard hadn't been handsome in the traditional sense, even when he was younger, but he had a positive attitude about life that she loved. And he had va-voom if anyone did! His jumping jacks still gave her tingles.

"No, you're not gonna meet the famous Richard," Tee-John said. "Your gift is a visit to a reenactment type event in Baton Rouge called, 'The War Years: A Celebration.'"

"Big whoop! Another Civil War re-enactment! When are Southerners gonna realize they lost that war? And why would ya imagine I'd be interested? You'd think I lived back then, the way some folks keep bringin' it up. 'Didja ever meet Jefferson Davis, Tante Lulu? Ha, ha, ha!' I ain't that old!"

Etienne muttered something that sounded like "Wanna bet?"

She turned and threatened to swat "Call me Steve" with her St. Jude fan, then told Tee-John, "Besides, ya keep tellin' me it's politically incorrect ta refer ta Northerners as Damn Yankees anymore. So, why we gonna celebrate that war again? We, fer certain, cain't be wavin' no Confederate flags, 'less we wanna be called big-hots."

Tee-John was laughing so hard he'd probably be peeing his pants. "You mean bigot, auntie. Not big-hot."

"I know what a bigot is, fool."

"Why do you bother correcting her?" Celine asked her husband, as if Louise wasn't even there.

Actually, Celine, and all the other LeDeux women for that matter—Sylvie, Rachel, Val, and Charmaine—were kind of mad at Louise, claiming that she had put a curse on them to make them all pregnant at this late stage in their lives. All Louise did was make a chance remark to St. Jude, in their hearing, that it would be nice to have more babies around.

Last summer, they were sure they were all breeding, then the next month they weren't, then they were, now no one was sure. Samantha was the only one not complaining, but she and Daniel were just getting started

How they could blame her for their wonky cycles was beyond Louise. It was all up to God...and St. Jude, of course. And, besides, everyone knew children were a blessing, not a curse.

In any case, Louise ignored Celine's snarkiness and continued, "As fer grown men playin' war games with antique guns? Pffft! And I ain't gonna sit around watchin' grown men whistle 'Dixie,' either, like we did at the Shrimp Festival last year."

Celine kept trying to interrupt her, and finally got a few words in. "Not that war, Tante Lulu."

"And, FYI, I don't think there were many Johnny Rebs

who took the time to whistle during the Civil War," Tee-John added, before she shut them both up.

"Do ya think I'm a total idjit? I'd like ta f. y. i. ya with my f. a. n."

Tee-John grinned.

Celine explained with a long sigh, as if Louise was the idjit in this car, and not them, "This is about the World War II era. There will be all kinds of venues related to the 1940s. Music, clothing, movies, dances, everything involving the home front."

Tee-John backed his wife up by telling Louise, "You're always tellin' us stories about that time, when you were single. We thought you'd enjoy it."

"Hmpfh! How'd ya hear about this?"

"A brochure came into the newspaper office, and I volunteered to cover the event." Celine was a feature reporter for the *Times Picayune* in New Orleans. "It's the first ever for Loo-zee-anna, but these kind of World War II celebrations are very popular all over the world, especially in Britain."

"Isn't there a World War II museum in Nawleans?" Louise asked.

"Yes, but this is different," Celine said.

"People want to go back to a time when life was simpler and country pride was at a high," Tee-John elaborated.

"Ya mean like Donald Trump wantin' ta make America proud again?"

"Not even close," Tee-John said with a laugh. "The 1940s were a time of austerity, as you well know. And people showed their pride and did their part by planting Victory Gardens, home canning, using ration books, buying war bonds."

"I still have a garden, and I still can fruit and vegetables," Louise said. "Big deal!"

Tee-John was the one sighing now. "We figured you were a young woman back then, and this event would bring back memories."

He had no idea! The years from 1942 to 1944 were the happiest and most tragic of her life, leading to what she called her Big Grief. She would never forget. And she didn't need any old war fair to jog her memories.

"It'll be fun," Celine said.

I'd rather stick needles in my eyes or watch a cypress tree grow.

"I hope they have tanks. I always wanted to climb into one of those tanks and shoot off a dozen rounds. Bam, bam, bam!" Steve/Etienne said.

"Don't ya dare climb up on any machinery," Tee-John warned. "You're already grounded fer that tattoo incident."

Tante Lulu chuckled. It was payback time for Tee-John, the wildest boy in the bayou. "Talk about bein' grounded, I remember the time ya went ta that clothing-optional party, Tee-John, when ya were little more'n Etienne's age."

"Auntie!" Etienne protested. "Call me Steve."

Tee-John groaned. "Did you hafta mention that party?" Celine laughed.

"Whoa!" Etienne hooted. "Tell me more."

"It wasn't clothing-optional, it was underwear-optional," Tee-John corrected.

"Oh, that's better. Not!" Celine remarked.

"I'm not wearing any underwear," Etienne informed them all.

Every person in the car looked at the boy, even his father through the rearview mirror, and the two "robots" in the way-back who pretended to be brain dead from cell phoneitis, but, apparently, heard everything. But no one said anything. What *could* you say to that?"

Doesn't it hurt?" Rob asked finally. "One time I went ta

school without my underwear 'cause my Superman tightie whities were dirty, and the zipper on my jeans chafed my tooter somethin' awful."

"Ya shoulda put some of my snake oil ointment on it," Louise advised.

"Ouch!" Etienne said. "You're supposed ta arrange yer goodies ta the side."

"Goodies? Eew!" Annie observed.

"Oh," was Rob's reaction. "How do ya do that arrangin' thing?"

"That's enough on the subject," Tee-John ordered.

"Talk about!" Louise remarked.

And Celine smacked her son on the shoulder.

"What did I do?" Etienne asked, but he was grinning like a pig in honey-coated slop.

When they parked in the State Fairgrounds lot, a huge banner did, indeed, announce, "The War Years: A Celebration," and Louise thought of something. "Y'know, Tee-John, lots of pacifists would be offended at a celebration of that war. It wasn't all swing music and pretty hairdos. There was some grim stuff goin' on back then. Yessirree. Like the Holocaust and Hiroshima, not ta mention all the soldiers that got killed." Including one near and dear to her own heart, she couldn't help but think. "'Course, we dint know 'bout the concentration camps and big bombs and all that till the end."

"I can answer that," Celine said.

Surprise, surprise!

"The event promoters put out a disclaimer ahead of time, stating that the war itself wasn't being celebrated, but the home front and the culture of the times," Celine went on.

Doesn't she always? Go on, and on, and on.

"In fact, they're making every effort to show respect for

those who died and the vets who survived with special activities, like an honor guard of remaining World War II veterans, a D-Day commemoration, and so on."

"You're right, though, auntie. We shouldn't look at the war with rose-colored glasses," Tee-John said, as he helped her out from the high seat. She was barely five feet tall in her bare feet. Auto makers were prejudiced against short people, if you asked her. She used to be five-foot-three... well, five-foot-two-and-a-half, but somehow the inches were disappearing, along with her boobs and butt.

Immediately, Annie took her one hand and Rob, the other. They really were sweet children. Maybe these two wouldn't turn out as wild as Tee-John and Etienne. And Celine wasn't so bad, either, Louise had to admit, especially if she could raise up three good children like these three. Or put up with Tee-John's antics, truth to tell.

Hundreds, maybe thousands, of people were strolling about the grounds. They followed the crowds.

A map of the fairgrounds showed where particular booths were situated, like vintage clothing, hair styling, music, movies, kitchen gadgets, food, Victory Gardens, toys, penny arcades, ration books, tea rooms, and picture booths. There would be a parade of classic cars later in the day.

"Lillian is a classic. She could be in the parade," Louise said.

"She isn't old enough, auntie," Tee-John said.

Louise didn't hear that very often, about herself anyway.

Despite what Celine had said, there was a lot of military stuff going on, Louise noticed, studying the roster some more, like a war bonds poster booth, displays of service uniforms, guns and ammo, aircraft, WACs, USOs, and historical booths that included a number of authors and the books they'd written about the war. Like the vintage cars, there would be a convoy of military vehicles.

At the far end of the grounds there was a stage where various swing bands would be playing, with a Bob Hope impersonator running the show. In addition, making an appearance would be Radio Josette, the Voice of the South, who had been popular with local servicemen back in the 40s.

"I thought Josette Sonnier died twenty years ago. Josie was usin' a walker at a fifty-year D-Day commemoration back in 1994. She mus' be ancient by now."

Etienne snickered behind her, as if her calling someone ancient was funny. She ignored him, for now, and explained, "Josie was a beauty, but mostly the fellows loved her 'cause she had this soft, sexy voice with a Southern accent. Made the homesick soldiers feel like there was allus someone waitin' fer them ta come back after the war."

To demonstrate, she lowered her voice and imitated Josie's usual greeting to her radio fans. "Hel-lo, boys! This is Radio Jo-sette comin' ta y'all from Loo-zee-anna. I've got somethin' fer ya, fellas, y'hear?"

Etienne wasn't snickering now. In fact, he was staring googly-eyed at her, while Tee-John was laughing like a drunk hyena.

But then, their attention was diverted to her niece Charmaine who'd joined them after emerging from a pick-up truck with the logo "Triple L Ranch," along with her husband Raoul "Rusty" Lanier and their daughter Mary Lou. Rusty and Mary Lou wore typical cowboy/cowgirl attire...denim pants and shirts, well-worn boots and hats. But Charmaine...Lordy, Lordy!...was dressed like a 1940s pin-up. And, believe it or not, Louise knew a lot about 1940s pin-ups. It didn't matter that Charmaine had hit the forty mark by now. As a former Miss Louisiana, she had an image to maintain. Face it, she was still hot as Cajun Lightning, or Tabasco sauce, the South's contribution to the world of spice.

Charmaine must have inherited Louise's genetic taste for outrageousness because she was wearing red, high-heeled, peep-toe pumps with seamed stockings. A white blouse with shoulder pads, unbuttoned to expose her famous cleavage, was tucked into a slim—very slim—black skirt that hugged her butt cheeks. A wide, red patent-leather belt cinched in her waist. Her long, black, wavy hair was tucked behind one ear and hung over the other eye, Veronica Lake style, topped by a pert little red pillbox hat with a half veil. Her make-up was expertly applied as usual to look natural, except for her favorite Crimson Fire lipstick. There wasn't a woman alive who could do justice to shiny red lipstick like Charmaine.

Rusty, the handsomest Cajun man to walk on two feet (everyone said so), looked as if he'd like to eat her up, like he always did. Crazy in love with his wife the boy had been for twenty years now.

If Charmaine was preggers, she sure was hiding it.

And there came Remy and his family...some of them anyways. There were a whole passel of them, including Andy LeDeux, the football player, who immediately had fans surrounding him, asking for autographs. Remy would have been just as good looking as Rusty, except, as a pilot during Desert Storm, he'd suffered massive burns, but only on one side of his body, forehead to toes. A shame, that! But he'd survived, that was the most important thing. Besides, to her, and to his adoring wife Rachel, he was still good-looking. And a hero.

Despite all their children, mostly adopted, Louise knew that Remy and Rachel would welcome more. But then, Rachel wasn't looking any fatter, either.

Her oldest nephew, Luc, and his wife Sylvie came, too, with their three daughters. Next to Tee-John, Luc was her favorite. As a young boy, he'd practically raised his brothers in a rusted-out trailer with no running water. Louise had rescued the boys from their abusive father, that devil Valcour LeDeux, and saved herself in the process.

Luc had a vasectomy a few years back. What a joke it would be on him if God...or St. Jude...stuck out a big toe and tripped him up! If God could raise the dead, he could surely undo a few of man's snips.

Finally came René and his two kids, Jude and Louise. Louise had a particular affection for these two little ones... Louise because the little girl was her namesake, and Jude because he was named after her favorite saint.

René's wife Val, a lawyer, was in court this morning, representing a woman accused of assaulting her low-life drunk of a husband. "Some men just need killing" was considered a legal defense in some parts of Louisiana. Or, "Some lowlifes jist need a good whompin'," Louise often said.

Val was the one the most upset with Louise over this whole I'm pregnant/I'm not pregnant issue. Val was the type of woman who thought she could control her life, without any help from Above, or even from down the bayou, meaning Louise.

René, an environmentalist and teacher, was also a musician—a member of the Swamp Rats, a popular bayou band. He headed immediately for the booth showcasing music of the World War II era. Old vinyl records and albums were being sold to a long line of customers, which was surprising since everyone today seemed to be getting their music from wires hanging from their ears. She wondered how anyone could play these records since stereos were obsolete. Heck, even eight-track tape players, cassettes, and CDs were outdated. *Too bad! It's a cryin' shame that we live in a throwaway society now. Toss it out if it shows any age. In fact, they'd throw old people out, too, if they could.*

But wait, the vendor was also selling antique record players, as well as modern reproductions, some of them inside actual furniture, like those old stereo cabinets, one of which she still had in her living room. Maybe the young'uns in her family would stop making fun of her after seeing this.

Another booth displayed collectible Bakelite radios. She had one of those, too—a Philco tabletop model that still played just fine.

The music was a wonderful backdrop for this event, but it caused the fine hairs to stand out all over her body, and she felt kind of lightheaded. She held onto Charmaine's arm as they walked along. The old sappy favorites, like "Stardust," "I'll Be Seeing You," and "Sentimental Journey," and even the more upbeat ones, like "Chattanooga Choo-Choo," and "Boogie Woogie Bugle Boy," they all triggered memories almost too painful to bear. Louise realized that she'd unconsciously avoided those songs over the decades in favor of the traditional French Cajun music, or zydeco, of the bayou. Now she knew why.

Etienne...rather, Steve...went off with his Daddy to look at all the military stuff, including, yes, a few tanks. Tee-John probably accompanied him so he wouldn't really climb into one of the things.

Next up was a booth about Victory Gardens and home canning. Hah! Cajuns, ever frugal, knew all about the benefits of raising their own food. There was even a booth about bayou animals, how to catch and cook them, including squirrels, raccoons, snakes...and gators, of course.

"There's a trend toward austerity t'day," Charmaine told her, using the same word Tee-John had, back in the car. "People wanna go back ta simpler lifestyles. Avoid processed foods and red meat. Live off the land, completely."

"Whass wrong with a supermarket once in awhile?" Louise asked. "And ain't nothin' like a rare roast beef with sides of okra and dirty rice."

"I cain't argue with that, livin' on a ranch and all. Right, Rusty?" Charmaine asked.

But Rusty and Mary Lou had already moved on to the next booth where an old-fashioned wringer-type washing machine was being demonstrated.

"I remember those. What a pain in the hiney they were! Took half a day jist ta do a little laundry. 'Course, Monday was allus wash day. And we allus had red beans an' rice simmerin' on the stove on Mondays 'cause it took no trouble."

Rob and Annie were fascinated by a Pez booth with samples of hundreds of the candy dispensers. An old Woolworth sign advertised them for ten cents each. She could only imagine what those early ones were worth today.

Cigarette girls walked around the grounds with trays held by a neck strap. Camels, Lucky Strikes, Pall Malls, Raleighs. They were probably empty packs, considering their reputation as "coffin nails," but there was no question they had been popular back in the day. She'd smoked a few herself, when she'd thought they made her look older and more sophisticated.

Separate booths dealt with ration books, Spam, Griswold cast-iron pans, and kitchen gadgets. Louise had to explain to Mary Lou the purpose of ice picks, hand-cranked meat grinders, and treadle sewing machines.

All the women and girls were fascinated by the vintage clothing on display. Both Sylvie and Rachel sat down to have their hair styled in "Victory Rolls" that ran from one ear, along the nape, to the other ear, with center parts, or cute bangs across their foreheads. Still others had their hair done into an "up-do."

Meanwhile, among the crowds, Celine pointed out that there were educators here who wanted to impart information about the era (the event organizers, historical societies, professors, and authors), men who liked boy toys (the military paraphernalia, in particular), and the promenaders (military re-enactors and people who just loved the attire of that time period, like Charmaine). Occasional World War II vets also hobbled about. Actually, veterans of other wars, as well.

Louise was particularly touched when she noticed some fellows in the old white "crackerjack" uniforms of the sailors, complete with the "Dixie Cup" or "gob" hats that could be molded to a rakish angle. The memories they triggered caused her heart to constrict so tight she could barely breathe.

"Are you all right?" Tee-John asked, coming to stand beside her. Apparently he and Etienne were done ogling the war planes and tanks.

"I'm fine," she replied, but looped her arm in his as they moved along.

"Holy shit!" Etienne said suddenly.

"Watch yer language." His father smacked him on his shoulder.

"Sorry," Etienne apologized, though he didn't look sorry at all. Instead, he pointed to a tent that had a display of 40s pin-up posters and magazine covers, including some by the famous painter Alberto Vargas.

"Lookee there, Tante Lulu was a centerfold."

"She was not!" Tee-John declared, giving his son another smack.

"Yes, I was," Tante Lulu said.

"Told ya!" Etienne hooted. "That chick up there looks jist lak Tante Lulu in that graduation picture on her dresser...the one in a silver frame. Y'know the one I mean, Daddy. She's wearin' a red dress and high heels and holdin' a diploma."

"I'll be damned!" Tee-John muttered.

Everyone in her family who'd gathered to see what the problem was turned as one to stare at her, up at the posters, then back at her.

"I was a pin-up, not a centerfold," Louise amended.

Luc groaned.

Tee-John laughed.

"Lemme see," Charmaine said, pushing her way forward. Then, examining the two posters in questions, she remarked, "Wow! You were a real beauty, auntie. Bet I could do one of these pin-up pictures. What do you think, Rusty?"

Rusty just made a gurgling sound.

"All of those pin-up artists made the women look like they had perfect figures, almost too perfect. There probably isn't a female alive with breasts so perky and waists so small. It was almost misogynistic and sexist, really. Worse than Barbie dolls," Celine informed them all.

Did I mention Celine is a know-it-all, bless her heart? "Bull-pucky!" Louise countered.

"Get out of there," Celine hissed as Etienne moved farther inside the tent, getting an eyeful of what would certainly appeal to an adolescent boy. To men, too, truth to tell. "Women don't really look like that," she continued to instruct her son. "It's just a male fantasy."

"God bless fantasies," Tee-John murmured as his eyes swept the array of posters.

Celine glared at him.

He waggled his eyebrows at her. "Hey, darlin', if I buy you one of those garter belts being sold back there with a pair of seamed stockings, I could take your picture with my cell phone, and—"

"Grow up!" Celine said.

"Never!" Tee-John and Louise hooted at the same time.

Celine had to smile then, shaking her head at the two of them.

Then Tee-John put his arm around his wife's shoulders and tugged her closer to his side, kissing the top of her head. She could hear him whisper, "You look better than any of these models, babe."

What a charmer!"

What's the difference," Etienne asked Louise, "between a centerfold and a pin-up?"

"The difference is clothes," Tante Lulu explained, following after Etienne. There was nothing but LeDeuxs in the big tent now. "Pin-ups wore clothes, centerfolds were buck nekkid. Mostly." She was peering closely at the two posters in question. She remembered when she'd had them done. Originally, she'd just wanted a racy picture to give to her fiancé, Phillipe Prudhomme, before he went away, but the painter, an associate of Vargas, Emmanuel Delgado, had convinced her to do several others, which had been used in a series of pin-up calendars sold in military canteens around the world.

One of the posters showed Louise wearing a red silk robe that exposed one leg up to the thigh and a cleavage no real woman ever had; in it, she posed on a pink chaise lounge, with her back arched so that her long, dark hair, like Charmaine's Veronica Lake 'do, hung back almost to the floor. Her hair hadn't been that long, either. Another bit of artistic license. On the other poster, she wore a strapless white bathing suit and white high-heeled pumps, posed against a boat. Perched on her up-do hairstyle, ala Judy Garland or Joan Crawford, was a white sailor cap.

"I looked good, dint I?" she said to Tee-John.

"Damn good! You actually appear tall in that one. At least five-seven, or –eight."

"Oh, that was a trick all the pin-up painters did at that time. They wanted tall women, of course, but they had ways ta make us shorter ladies have longer legs. Like that picture shopping they do t'day."

"She means photoshopping," Celine told Tee-John.

"I know what it means," Louise snapped.

The owner of the tent, overhearing their conversation, came up to them and asked Louise, "Would you mind autographing a few of your posters?"

"Sure," she said.

Actually, her family members bought most of them, wanting evidence, no doubt, that their outrageous Tante Lulu had been outrageous, even back then.

"What do you say to a little lunch?" Luc suggested. "There's a food tent over there. Aunt Hattie's Tea Room. Looks like fun. Scones with clotted cream and lemon curd. Crustless finger sandwiches. Yum."

She didn't know if Luc was serious or poking fun. Whatever. Louise wasn't really hungry, but she'd been on her feet all morning, and she'd welcome a little break. They had to pass the USO tent before they got to the tea room.

Sylvie linked arms with her on one side and Luc on the other. "Did you ever go to one of these?" Sylvie asked her.

"Are ya kiddin'? I lived in those canteens durin' the war. It's where I first met Phillipe. Well, not really 'met' fer the first time. We knew each other from down the bayou when we were both young'uns, but Phillipe was six years older than me. It was in the Nawleans USO where we got t'gether—really got t'gether, if ya get my meanin'."

"We got your meanin', auntie. No explanation needed," Luc said.

"Are ya funnin' me again?"

"Me?" He looked at her with mock innocence.

"Fool!" she said and glanced toward the USO tent as they passed.

Then stopped dead in her tracks and did a double take.

Disengaging herself from Luc and Sylvie, she moved hesitantly into the tent where many pictures of USOs from Louisiana were displayed. It was the black-and-white photo, enlarged to poster size, which showed her and Phillipe slow-dancing at the Fort Polk USO New Year's Eve dance in 1943.

Phillipe hadn't been overly tall. Only about five foot ten, but with her high-heeled pumps and dancing on her tippy toes, there had only been a few inches difference in their height. She, wearing her then-favorite tea-length gown of red chiffon, was gazing up at him with adoration. He, in his Navy dress uniform, Cajun to the core, was smiling down at her. A couple in love, no doubt about it.

Louise remembered that night as if it were yesterday. The band had been playing "Star Dust." She could still smell his Aqua Velva, and her own musky Tabu. Still feel his nighttime stubble against her cheek. The press of his one hand against her lower back, the other hand holding her palm against his heart, thus displaying her new engagement ring, which had been a Christmas present. The whisper of his "I love you, *chère*" against her ear.

That's when all the events of the day, the nostalgia, the jarred memories, good and so painful they still made her heart hurt in her chest, took their toll. There was only so much a lady could take.

Louise, for only the second time in her life, fell into a dead faint.

Get your copy of *When Lulu was Hot* today!

EXCERPT FROM BAYOU ANGEL

The angel was wild tonight...

*A*ngel Sabato stood at the edge of the dance floor like a dunce, shaking in his thousand-dollar Tres Outlaws boots as he watched the redhead shake her booty to the beat of "Wild Thing." For an ex-nun, she sure had moves.

Ironically, he was the one feeling wild. His hands were clammy, his heart was thumping—*da dump, da dump, da dump*—and, truth to tell, he was scared spitless. Tonight was going to be the night. Do-or-die time.

It was ridiculous, really. He was thirty-four years old. He'd been around the block so many times there were probably street signs named after him. At the least, his "tread marks" were notorious. Shyness wasn't even in his vocabulary. After all, he was the dick-for-brains who'd once bared it all for *Playgirl* magazine.

Just then the redhead in question, Grace O'Brien, noticed him and smiled widely, crooking a forefinger for him to come out and join her.

Not a chance.

It wasn't dancing he had on his mind.

She said something to her partner, one of the young LeDeuxs...a freshman at LSU. Then she left the kid behind and snaked a slow, sensuous boogie toward him, her twinkling green eyes holding his the entire time, her arms held out in front of her, fingers beckoning. She must be half plastered or, more likely, in a teasing mood.

He was not in the mood for teasing.

"Yo, matey," she drawled at him.

This was the tail end of the Pirate Ball. It was being held here in Houma, Louisiana, to celebrate the successful search by Jinx, Inc., a treasure-hunting company, for Jean Lafitte's hidden gold. Thus the silly pirate talk. Not to mention silly pirate costumes.

He and Grace had worked on the Jinx team's Pirate Project these past weeks. Before that they'd been professional poker players. And before that, Grace had been a nun, and he had been in the navy, then construction, and...well, a lot of things.

She was dancing around him now, dressed in a saucy tavern-wench costume with a jagged knee-length hem, while he was in a puffy shirt tied with a red sash. *Jerry Seinfeld would be so proud of me.*

When he pretended to ignore her sexy dancing, she grabbed his upper arm and attempted to tug him forward. Being about seventy-five pounds heavier at six-foot-one to her measly five-foot-five, he was pretty much immovable.

She put her hands on her hips and glared at him. "Come out here and shake a peg leg, you randy buccaneer."

He had to grin at that. "Who says I'm randy?"

"You're always randy."

"And you know this...how?"

"All the satisfied smiles I've seen on women exiting your revolving bedroom door the past ten years."

"You noticed?"

"Stop changing the subject. I wanna dance."

"Are you blitzed?" he asked with a laugh.

"Just a little," she slurred.

Luckily, the DJ changed the music to a different pace. Now Mariah Carey was urging "Touch My Body."

He opened his arms to Grace and adjusted her so that her arms were around his neck and his hands were linked behind her waist, just above her butt. And yes, Mariah, he had touching in mind. Touching Grace.

"I'm flying back to Jersey early tomorrow morning. I need to talk to you," he said into her hair, which smelled like apples, or was it peaches? Some kind of frickin' fruit, anyway.

"Uh-huh. I'm listening," she replied, definitely not listening as she nuzzled her face into the crook of his neck, inadvertently pressing her belly against the crotch of his tights.

Yeah, he was wearing XXX-sized tights. With testosterone-induced hysterical irrelevance, he mused that the guys back in his old gang in Newark would get a kick out of him in latex, unless it were of the prophylactic kind. Or was that spandex? Spandex, latex, whatever! That was beside the point. *Call me crazy, but did she just lick my ear?*

Blood drained from his head and slam-dunked into sex central. For a second, he thought his knees might give out.

"Not here," he gurgled. "Let's go outside for a walk, down by the bayou. Better yet, I'll take you back to your hotel room."

"I already checked out. I'll be staying with Tante Lulu from now on." She leaned her head back to look at him. "You sound serious."

"I am serious, babe." He wondered if she was aware that when she arched back like that it caused his erection to rub against her belly button, which was exposed by her low-riding wench skirt. And that was damn serious.

"You can drive me to the cottage. Let's go tell Tante Lulu that I'm leaving."

"So, you're staying with that Cajun dingbat, huh?" he asked, arm looped over her shoulder as they walked to the other side of the hall, where Tante Lulu was chattering away to some guy in a frock coat and tricorne hat. At least he wasn't wearing tights.

Louise Rivard, better known as Tante Lulu, was the craziest old woman he'd ever met. But she was a noted *traiteur,* or folk healer, and Grace had decided to apprentice herself to the fruitcake in hopes of learning more about the healing arts. Really, Grace's life was like a pendulum swinging from one extreme to the other. Nun to poker player to treasure hunter to healer. He couldn't wait to see where she landed next, as long as she took him along for the ride.

"Don't call her a dingbat." Grace turned slightly and swatted him on the chest, then grinned. "Even if she is a dingbat."

"Grace...Angel...hope y'all had a good time t'night." Tante Lulu was dressed as a senior citizen pirate gal. A scary sight, to be sure—she was ninety years old, give or take. No one knew for sure. She eyed them suspiciously when Grace told her she would be leaving with him. Grace was oblivious to that pointed look, which took in his arm on Grace's shoulder, but he could practically see the matchmaking wheels churning in Tante Lulu's little brain. "That full moon t'night, she is purty enough to make a cat smooch a hound dog."

"Huh?" Grace said.

"Welcome to TanteLuluville," he muttered under his breath, then smiled.

"Ya got a hope chest?" Tante Lulu asked Angel just before they walked away. Tante Lulu had a tradition of making hope chests for the men in her family, or male friends of the family, just before the "thunderbolt of love" hit them.

Hah! He had news for the Louisiana love bug. That thunderbolt had done its business with him a long time ago.

"So, what did you want to talk to me about?" Grace asked, once they were sitting in his rental car back in Tante Lulu's cottage driveway. She didn't seem so tipsy anymore.

A full moon allowed him to see Grace's face. She was concerned. For him.

"I want you to come back with me, sweetheart." Well, that was laying his cards on the table from the get-go.

She frowned. "Back to your motel room?"

"No. I mean, yeah, that would be great, but I meant, fly back to the East Coast with me in the morning. Come with me and the Jinx team to Germany for our next project." He gulped. "Just come with me, that's all."

"I don't understand. You know I quit treasure hunting. It was never intended to be more than a one-shot deal for me. I've already explained why I'm staying here." She moved closer and accidentally put a hand on his thigh.

Big mistake, that.

He picked her up by the waist and laid her across his lap, her head cradled over his left elbow. "This isn't about treasure hunting, or folk healing, or any other damn profession. It's about you and me." He leaned down, kissed her lightly on the lips, and whispered against her gaping mouth, "I love you, Grace."

She squirmed into a sitting position on his lap. "I love you, too, sweetie. You're my best friend."

"Dammit! That's not what I'm talking about. I'm *in love* with you, have been for a long time."

A stunned silence was not what he was looking for here.

"You're kidding, right? What's the punch line? You gonna tell some lame nun joke?" She nipped at his lower lip with her teeth as punishment.

Angel jerked backward, though he didn't release her from his embrace. It was true, he had been teasing Grace with nun jokes for ages, even though she hadn't been a nun for ages, but not now. "This is not a joke, Grace."

She stared at him for a long moment. "Sex. All this forced celibacy while trapped out in the bayou must have turned you horny. You want to have sex with me." Grinning, she taunted him with that last accusation.

"No! I mean, yes. Here's the deal: I don't want sex for sex's sake, as in any ol' female would do. I want to *make love* with you. But that's not all I want. C'mon," he said, opening the car door and hauling her outside. *Oh, God! I'm blowing it. What the hell is wrong with me?* "Let's walk."

"You're scaring me, Angel."

"I'm scaring myself," he muttered as he linked his hand with hers and led her onto Tante Lulu's back porch facing the bayou. Once they were leaning against the rail, he raised their linked hands and kissed her knuckles.

"Oooh, you are smooth."

"You have no idea." Something occurred to him then, related to her mentioning going back to his motel room. *"Would* you have sex with me? Just like that?" He snapped his fingers. "Friends with benefits?"

"I don't know. Maybe."

Angel was both angry and intrigued.

"Actually, I probably wouldn't. Even half drunk. You and I have been friends for a long time. I wouldn't want to do anything to ruin that."

He shook his head. "Not anymore."

She frowned. "What do you mean?"

"I mean, friendship isn't enough anymore. Haven't you felt it, too, Gracie, these weeks we've been here in Louisiana? Those LeDeuxs are crazy as coots, but they're a close-knit family. They would do anything for each other. And you can just see the passion between the husbands and wives. Luc and Sylvie. Remy and Rachel. René and Val. Rusty and Charmaine. John and Celine. That's what I want."

"Passion?"

"Passion, yeah, but more than that."

"Family?" she said with an oddly sad sigh.

"Bingo. I want a woman to love who will love me back. And a home...a real home, not some luxury condo. And kids."

The more he explained himself, the stiffer she got. Then she started biting on her thumbnail, a nervous habit she'd been trying to break ever since he'd first met her. Angel sensed he was losing her bit by bit, but he didn't know how to fix it.

"You and I have no close family ties," she reminded him, pulling her hand out of his grasp and walking to the other end of the porch. He followed after her. "The LeDeuxs have family out the wazoo."

"We can make our own family. I love you, honey. That's what people in love do."

"Where is all this coming from?" Her voice was shrill with panic. "You never mentioned love before."

"It's been there for a long time. I just haven't had the nerve to say anything."

"You? Lacking nerve?"

He nodded. "But I had to say something now. This Amber Project—Jinx's next job—is going to take months, maybe even a year, and it'll be mostly on-site in Germany. We're searching for that famous Amber Room that the Nazis supposedly dismantled and hid. Definitely Jinx's most ambitious treasure hunt yet, and I want you to be there with me. As my wife. Doesn't a honeymoon in Europe sound great?" His heart was racing so fast it felt as if it might explode. Deep down, he sensed he was fighting a losing battle. How could he have misread her so badly?

"This is insane. You've never even kissed me...that way. You can't ask someone to marry you without even a proper kiss."

That was his cue. "I thought you'd never ask."

When she saw his slow grin and his equally slow approach, she stuttered, "That's not what—oh, good grief, what are you doing?"

"About to kiss you properly." Before she could blink, or tell him to get lost, he backed her up against the wall of the cottage, cupped her butt cheeks, raising her to just the right height on her tiptoes, spread her legs with his knees, anchored her with his belly against her belly, combed his fingers through her hair to hold her in place, then kissed her with all the love he'd been holding in for so long.

It should have been a gentle kiss, coaxing. An introduction. Something that said, "Hi! We've known each other forever, as friends, but this is how I really feel. I love you. Do you love me?"

Instead, his sex drive shot from zero to the speed of light in a nanosecond, and the gentle, coaxing kiss was anything but. It was hungry and demanding and said, "Oh, baby, I want you so bad. I can't wait, I can't wait, I can't wait—"

Just then, a loud bellow echoed behind them.

"*What* was that?" he asked, his head jerking back.

"An alligator, I think. Probably Remy's pet Useless. It's harmless."

An alligator? Close by? Harmless? He pressed his forehead against hers, both of them panting for breath.

"This is not the way I want to make love to you the first time, sweetheart. Come back to my motel room with me, and we can talk."

She tried to laugh but it came out choked. "I think we've done enough *talking*." Ducking under his arm, she stepped away.

Immediately, Angel sensed the tension in the air, and it wasn't a good tension. She put up a halting hand when he moved a step closer.

"Angel, I am not going to marry you, and we are not going to have a family together. It is just not going to happen. Ever."

"Why?"

"Because I'm not in love with you."

Angel had been playing poker for too many years not to read her "tells." He'd like to think she was lying through her teeth. She wasn't. How could he have interpreted her signals so wrong? "You don't mean that, Gracie." *Please, God, don't let her mean it.*

"Angel! Come on. I've seen you puking your guts out when you've drunk too much. That's a friend, not a lover."

He shrugged. "I've gone out and bought you tampons when you had an accident in white slacks. Didn't make me go 'eew!'"

"I saw you clipping your gross toenails in the kitchen."

He grinned. "You have funny-looking toes. The pinkies are crooked."

"You told me my toes were cute."

215

"They are cute. Crooked cute."

All this was just blowing smoke, in his opinion. Of no importance. Once again, he tried to move closer.

Once again, she put up a halting hand. "You've been the best friend I've ever had, but I don't feel *that way* about you. Really, I had no idea—"

"Your kiss," he said, indicating with a wave of his hand the section of porch they'd just left, "your kiss said something else."

There were tears in her eyes. "Sexual attraction fueled by too much alcohol."

"I'm not buyin' it."

"You have to. Besides, there are things in my past...things you don't know about me."

"Hell, I have secrets in my past, too. Big deal!" He waited a moment, then asked, "What things?"

"I can't say. Just know that I have good reasons for saying that you and I will never be a family, aside from my just thinking of you as a friend—my best friend."

"Well, we're sure as hell not gonna continue being friends with this between us now."

"Oh, Angel."

"I'm leaving, Gracie. Are you coming with me?"

She shook her head, unable to speak.

"So be it. I doubt we'll be seeing each other again. I don't do begging very well." He stared at her, then added, "I love you, babe. I really do."

~

Two weeks later, and the news heard 'round the world, or at least, down the bayou...

GRACE WAS IN THE PANTRY, using a mortar and pestle to grind dried herbs for Tante Lulu's amazing medicinal potions.

Pennyroyal, horehound, sassafras, and catnip, which could be brewed into a tea and used for coughs.

Yarrow and jimsonweed to go in poultices.

Sumac for arthritis.

So many healing uses for nature's bounty. And any one of them could have varying uses, depending on the stage of development—seed, root, flower, or full-grown plant.

Dust motes danced on the stream of sunlight coming from the lone window. Through the screen she could hear a hundred bayou birds join together, celebrating their unique habitat. As she worked, she glanced over at the floor-to-ceiling shelves, neatly lined with dozens of glass bottles. Some of them were baby food jars. Some jelly jars. Even old green mason jars with lead lids. Each had its own label. Each followed specific ingredients for one of the noted *traiteur's* remedies—983, at last count—that were outlined, longhand, in numerous journals that had their own shelf. No computer software for her boss. *No-siree,* as Tante Lulu would say.

The pungent odors in the room, the feeling of history, the warmth of Tante Lulu's essence: all these things contributed to Grace's sense of well-being. She was at peace. Not happy, precisely, but finally she was where she belonged.

A psychiatrist would have a field day with her history. From promiscuous teenager to nun. Nun to poker player. Poker player to treasure hunter. Treasure hunter to folk healer. Still, she'd found a place that felt safe and promising to her.

The only thing interfering with her happiness was Angel. Her heart grieved at the hole her former friend had created in her life by his absence. The louse hadn't called her. Probably his pride had kicked in. And she wasn't going to call him. That would give him false expectations. Even if she was in love—and she wasn't—there were other reasons why a future with him would be out of the question.

"Yoo-hoo!"

Tante Lulu must be back from her trip to Boudreaux's General Store. Her nephew John LeDeux had picked her up an hour ago.

Grace finished bottling her concoction, dusted her hands off, and walked into the kitchen, where Tante Lulu and John were unloading armfuls of overflowing paper bags. Both of them glanced at her. And said nothing.

"What?" It was obvious by the way they avoided direct eye contact that something was wrong.

"Ah, Gracie, bless yer heart," Tante Lulu said, reaching up to pat her cheek.

Now Grace was really frightened. "Tell me."

"Tee-John was talkin' ta Ronnie this mornin'," Tante Lulu started to explain, then stopped, turning to her nephew for help.

Tee-John, or Little John, was the nickname that had been given to John LeDeux when he was a kid, and much smaller than his six foot or so in height now.Ronnie was Veronica Jinkowsky, owner of Jinx, Inc., the treasure hunting company.

"Oh, my God! Is it Angel? Has something happened to him?"

"You could say that," John drawled out. The sympathy in his dark Cajun eyes caused alarm bells to go off in her head and her heart rate to accelerate alarmingly.

"He got married yesterday," John told her. "To an airline stewardess he met on the way to Germany. Talk about!"

Grace plopped down into the kitchen chair, stunned. *So*

much for true love! She tried her best not to be hurt. After all, she was the one who'd sent him away, but the tears came anyway.

They would never renew their friendship now.

She tried to tell herself it was best this way.

Get your copy of *Bayou Angel* today!

ABOUT THE AUTHOR

Sandra Hill is the best-selling author of almost fifty novels and the recipient of numerous awards. She has appeared on many bestseller lists, including the *New York Times* and *USA Today*.

Readers love the trademark humor in her books, whether the heroes are Vikings, Cajuns, Navy SEALs, treasure hunters, or vangels (Viking vampire angels), and they tell her so often, sometimes with letters that are laugh-out-loud funny. In addition, her fans feel as if they know the characters in her books on a personal basis, especially the outrageous Tante Lulu.

At home in central Pennsylvania with her husband, four sons, a dog the size of a horse, six dogs belonging to her sons, and three grandchildren, Sandra is always busy. When she is not at their home, so close to the Penn State football stadium that she can hear the Blue Band practicing every night, she can be found relaxing at their Spruce Creek cottage.

Sandra is always on the lookout for new sources of humor. So be careful if you run into Sandra. What you say or do may end up in a book. If you want to take the chance, you can contact her at SandraHill.net. She loves to hear from her fans.

ALSO BY SANDRA HILL

Sandra Hill's Cajun Novels (In Order):

The Love Potion

Tall, Dark, and Cajun

The Cajun Cowboy

The Red-Hot Cajun

Pink Jinx

Pearl Jinx

Wild Jinx

So Into You (Bayou Angel)

Snow on the Bayou

The Cajun Doctor

Cajun Crazy

Cajun Persuasion

Novellas

"Jinx Christmas" in *A Dixie Christmas* Anthology

"Saving Savannah" in *Heart Craving* Anthology

When Lulu was Hot Prequel

Lulu's Recipe for Cajun Sass Prequel

Please note: Tante Lulu also appears as a secondary character in
these books:

Good Vampires Go to Heaven

Even Vampires Get the Blues

Kiss of Wrath

Kiss of Temptation

Made in the USA
Columbia, SC
29 April 2021